The Better Choice

KIERSTEN MODGLIN

www.kierstenmodglinauthor.com
Cover Design: Tadpole Designs
Editing: Three Owls Editing
Formatting: Tadpole Designs
First Print Edition: 2019
First Electronic Edition: 2019

"Kiersten Modglin brings an interesting romance story to the table with her classic twists that leave you in a "WTF-like state."

Modglin always brings a story full of edge of your seat feelings. While her thrillers have more twists to try and anticipate, her romances have enough to keep you reeling for days after finishing."

BOOKS AND BABBLE BLOG

To my husband, Michael, for giving me the whole fairytale.
You were the best choice I ever made.

CHAPTER ONE

B lythe had no idea what was coming for her that morning. It felt so normal—a morning like any other.

"Beckett, come eat your breakfast, sweetheart," she called toward the living room, watching as her son bounded into the kitchen, a stuffed dog in one hand. The dog was a present from his grandmother—his latest favorite, and it was evident by the stains that already needed to be washed out. "Here you go. Breakfast," she told him, patting the counter as he climbed up into his seat. "Set Scruffy down."

She heard footsteps headed down the stairs as her husband came into view. He was adjusting his shirt as he grabbed a piece of toast and kissed her lips. After all their years together, he still managed to send butterflies through her stomach with just a look.

"You look beautiful," he told her, his stubble scraping her skin as he cupped her ass and squeezed playfully.

She felt her face grow red, kissing him again and

handing over the mug of coffee she already had poured for him. "Big day today?" she asked.

He took a sip of coffee, inhaling sharply as it burned his tongue.

"Big day *always*," he said with a nod. "I've gotta meet with the client before we finish up the project. It's looking like," he paused to knock on wood, "we might actually finish up this one without incident."

Blythe nodded, watching Beckett as he smeared a bit of jam from the corner of his mouth to his cheek with the back of his hand. "Beck, use a napkin please, baby."

"I'm so proud of you," she said, looking back at her husband. He shrugged. It wasn't the first project he'd led, but it was still a significant one. And, though he wouldn't brag on himself, she would happily brag for him. He'd worked his ass off for that promotion, and it was well deserved.

Crap, she thought as she heard a knock on the door. Who in the world could possibly be visiting so early in the morning on a Thursday? She rolled her eyes at the thought of some of the neighborhood moms who would already have a yoga class in by now. He furrowed his brow at her, and she knew he was thinking the same thing.

They loved their home, truly they did, but sometimes they both longed for the anonymity that the city had once given them. The place where they didn't know anyone. The place where they wouldn't be bothered by anyone.

She walked to the door, patting Beckett's head, though he didn't seem fazed by the interruption. She felt her husband's hand on her back as they walked through the kitchen, then the living room, and into the foyer. She took a breath, in no way prepared for what would be waiting for her as she swung open the door.

The man in front of her was familiar. She recognized him instantly, though his face had aged significantly in just a few years. She sucked in a sharp breath, blinking heavily. What was happening? Her brain couldn't compute.

Her husband, who seemed equally shocked to see their visitor, cleared his throat and lowered his voice.

"What are you doing here?" he demanded.

The visitor grimaced, clearly not happy to be there either. "I'm here to see my son."

CHAPTER TWO

SIX YEARS EARLIER

T he masked man jerked the purse from her arm, not realizing it was thrown across her chest. He tried to run, practically dragging her as she attempted to pull the oversized purse back. It contained everything she owned—the only things of hers left in the world.

"Hey!" someone called from behind them, and she heard hurried footsteps headed their way. The mugger jerked, shoving his arm out and knocking her off her feet.

She fell to the ground with a thud, slamming her elbow onto the concrete and cursing. She saw her attacker running down the street, bag in hand, before turning left into the dark alley. She sighed heavily, feeling foolish and frustrated.

Day one in New York, and already she'd been mugged. *Face it*, her mother had been right. Small-town girls didn't belong in the city. Suddenly, she felt a hand slide under her arm and tensed up. She'd forgotten all about the man who'd attempted to save her. His face was near her ear. "Whoa, there, you okay?" he asked. He tried to help her stand.

She nodded, looking up to see the man standing behind her. He was tall, dark, and incredibly handsome. Dark brown eyes, shaggy brown hair that nearly covered them, and a leather jacket that fit him loosely over his tight jeans and boots. "Um, thank you, yeah, I'm okay," she said, dusting off the butt of her jeans as she stood.

He glanced at her elbow, wincing. "Ouch, that looks like it hurts," he said, pointing to the blood dripping onto the pavement. She hadn't realized she'd even been hurt until that moment, and suddenly the sharp pain ripped through her.

She nodded, holding her opposite sleeve under the wound. "Yeah, it does."

He nodded his head in the opposite direction. "I live right around the corner. I can get that cleaned up if you want."

She bit her lip, knowing it had to be a horrible decision. If she couldn't go home with a strange man in Darlington, she surely shouldn't be going home with a stranger in New York. But her arm hurt. And she was still a twenty-minute cab ride away from her aunt's house. Which meant she'd have to walk through the streets, bleeding all over the place until she found a place to buy some gauze and medical tape. Add that to the fact that she was dead broke without a purse and he was insanely gorgeous, and you can understand why she followed him back.

Or...maybe you wouldn't. Maybe she'd just lost that much blood.

Either way, within minutes, she was walking up the stairs to his apartment building. He turned around as they climbed the stairs, constantly checking on her. "You still okay?"

She nodded, applying pressure as she continued to lose blood. Finally, they reached his door and he turned the key. He didn't bother saying 'excuse the mess' like she was accustomed to in the South, though his place certainly *was* a mess. Empty beer bottles lined the countertop behind her, dress shirts had been thrown lazily over the back of the couch, and there was a pizza box on the coffee table. Maybe it was just a bachelor's pad. Blythe had never been in one, so she wouldn't know the difference.

The man held out his hand. "Wait here," he said, disappearing down a hallway and appearing a few moments later with a bottle of alcohol and some bandages. "I don't have a whole lot, but this should help until you can get home." He took hold of her arm, twisting it cautiously so he could see the wound. He pulled her toward the kitchen sink, which was just across the open room, and grabbed a towel from his drawer. He wiped her arm, stopping as she winced.

"It's okay," she assured him through gritted teeth, ignoring the sting as he poured the alcohol onto the cut. "What's your name, by the way?" she asked, feeling like she should at least know that.

He smiled up at her from behind a strand of dark hair. "Finn," he said. "I'm Finn."

Finn. She turned the name over in her head. It was unique. Unconventional. She wondered if it was short for something—Finley, perhaps. He didn't look like a Finley, but Finn seemed to fit. "Well, thank you, Finn, for saving me."

He let out a soft laugh as he wrapped the bandage around her arm. "I'm not sure I technically saved you, but I'm happy to help anyway..." He trailed off, raising his brow as if to ask for her name.

"Blythe," she introduced herself.

"Well, I'm happy to help, Blythe." His touch lingered on her arm, though he was done with the bandage at that point. He tucked a piece of his dark hair behind his ear, and she smiled at him, noticing the way his gaze burned into hers. *The smolder,* she would dub that look.

He let go of her arm suddenly, wadding up the paper from the bandage and tossing it into the trash. "So, do you live around here?"

She shook her head. "This is actually my first time in New York."

He nodded, as if she was confirming something he already suspected. "Nice. I figured. You seem...Southern."

"Well, that's not hard to assume, with the accent," she said, trying to mask it. "I'm definitely Southern. What about you? You're from here, obviously. But...have you always lived here?"

He smirked. "No, not always."

He wasn't giving her anything else, and neither was she. They were at a stand-off, staring into each other's eyes and feeling the electricity pulse between them. At least, *she* was feeling the electricity pulsing. Was it just her imagination?

He closed his eyes for a half-second, and when he opened them, his lips parted. Time seemed to stand still, as she, being the Southern Belle that she was, waited for him to make a move. He didn't. Instead, he cleared his throat.

"Well, I…um, I was going to go grab some dinner when I ran into you. Do you…want to join me?"

She took a breath, suddenly out of her trance. "Oh, I don't know."

"Come on," he dared her. "It's just dinner. Then I'll walk you to wherever you're staying."

She didn't agree, but before she knew it, he was leading her out of his apartment anyway, his hand on her arm. His touch felt good to a girl who'd been untouched for so long. She followed him down all four flights of stairs and back onto the street.

"So," he said, turning to look at her, "what do you like?"

The answer in her head was a resounding *'you,'* but that wasn't what he was asking.

———

AN HOUR LATER, they were finally sitting at a table in a small Italian restaurant where the owner knew Finn by name. A happy-looking waitress brought over a plate of bread and took their orders. Finn recommended a type of pasta and a drink she'd never heard of, and she gladly took his advice.

When the waitress left, Finn leaned forward, tearing

off a piece of bread and staring at her as he popped it into his mouth. "So," he said once his mouth was empty, "tell me what brought you to New York."

She laughed. "Ahh...The Big Apple?"

His forehead wrinkled in a playful scowl. "Yeah, no one calls it that."

"Point taken," she said.

"You didn't answer my question," he said, not buying into her distraction.

She nodded, taking in a breath. "Well, I'm from Texas."

"Of course you are," he muttered under his breath, not breaking eye contact.

"And, well, I grew up in a town near Austin...but my house burned down last year and took both of my parents with it."

His face remained still, though his eyes softened. "I'm so sorry, Blythe."

She nodded, used to empty apologies. It seemed like all anyone knew to say when they heard the news, and she guessed she couldn't blame them. What else was there to say, anyway? "Thank you," she said simply.

"So, you came to New York for a fresh start?"

She shrugged. "Well, Texas may be large, but Darlington is very small...and it starts to feel exceedingly so after a while. I got tired of everyone seeing me as 'that poor girl who lost her parents,' you know? It was hard enough without everyone around me knowing about it."

His eyes narrowed, lips in a thin line. "I know that feeling all too well."

"Oh really? You're a poor, small-town girl, too?" she joked.

She didn't expect a laugh, but when it came, it was warm and filled the space of the room. "Yeah, something like that," he said, raising his eyebrows as if her joke had surprised him.

"Well, anyway, my aunt lives just outside the city. She told me I could come stay with her for a while if I wanted. While I try to get everything figured out."

"What's...everything?"

"I mean, what I'm going to do next. I always thought I'd live in Texas my whole life. But now...I can do anything I want. It sounds freeing, but it's kind of terrifying."

"I get that," he agreed, and something told her he truly did. Before they could say anything else, the waitress appeared with their plates and drinks, setting them in front of the couple with a charming smile before disappearing toward the kitchen.

"This looks delicious," she said, picking up a fork.

"So, what do you want?" he asked, and for a moment she had to think about what he was asking.

"Oh, you mean in life?"

He smirked. "Yeah, in life."

"I have no idea," she answered honestly, shoving a forkful of food into her mouth. God, she was starving. "I'm just trying not to think about it. On top of trying not to think about how the hell I'm going to get away from my aunt as soon as possible."

"You two don't get along?"

"Oh, we get along fine. About as fine as can be expected."

"Meaning..." He trailed off, waiting for her to fill in

the blank she shouldn't have left.

She rolled her eyes. "Meaning my aunt thinks I'm a trollop."

He snorted, nearly inhaling his food. As he pulled the fork from his mouth, his eyes wide, he let out a scoff. "*Excuse me? A trollop?*"

She smiled, waving a hand over her head. "Unfortunately, yes. That's the exact word she used. I'm pretty sure she thinks I'm the devil incarnate coming to live at her house and bring her to the dark side. She's just...she's uber religious, and anyone who'd dare wear blue jeans must be up to *something naughty*," she said, imitating her aunt's nagging voice as best she could.

He took another bite, seemingly calm. "Well, lucky you, coming to New York then, huh? You'll fit right in."

She caught a twinkle in his eye that made her stomach lurch. Something told her she would *definitely* be fitting right in.

AT THE END of the date, Finn covered the bill, even though Blythe insisted she'd cover her half. Luckily he did, because, as she kept forgetting, her wallet was in her purse, which she remembered *again,* had been stolen.

They walked out of the restaurant together, his arm brushing hers occasionally in a way that made her wonder if he was trying to hold her hand.

"So, to your aunt's, then? Which way is that?"

She shook her head. "She lives outside of the city. I'll have to take a cab." She slapped her hand onto her forehead as soon as she'd said it. "Crap. No. I'll have to call her and see if she can come pick me up. No purse. Dammit. Welcome to New York, right?"

He smirked, running a hand through his hair. "That guy *was* a part of our welcoming committee, now that you mention it." He paused. "Hey, why don't you come back to my place for the night? *I don't mean that how it sounds,*" he said, though she'd never said she didn't want him to mean it exactly how it sounded—she was a *trollop*, after all. "I just assume that your aunt probably won't want to drive into the city so late. She doesn't exactly seem to like the nightlife crowd. You can call her and tell her where to pick you up tomorrow."

"Oh, no, honestly, I couldn't put you out like that," she said, trying to be polite, though she desperately wanted to say yes.

"It's fine," he said simply. "It makes the most sense, anyway. If you trust me."

She nodded, surprising herself as the truth slipped from her tongue. "I trust you."

BACK AT HIS place once again, he offered to let her sleep in his bed, which she promptly declined.

"I'm honestly not being...chivalrous or whatever. I'll sleep on the couch. It's just...I don't have extra bed stuff. Pillows or whatever. And I'm not going to make you sleep out here with nothing. I'll be fine. I usually crash on the couch, anyway."

She bit her lip. "Are you sure?" she asked.

He raised his eyebrows. "You aren't gonna steal from me, are ya?"

"What, and become a part of New York's welcoming committee? Honestly, the job didn't seem all that glamorous."

He laughed—*she loved the way he laughed at her jokes*—and rubbed a thumb over his lip, walking past her toward the bedroom. He pulled open a drawer and handed her a T-shirt and sweatpants. "Don't worry, they're clean."

She held them tightly to her chest, staring at the man who'd saved her life in more ways than one that day. "Thank you, Finn. For...everything."

"I didn't do much," he said simply. "Bathroom's there." He pointed to a door to his right. "You can wake me up if you need anything."

She nodded in agreement, watching as he walked out the door. Before it had closed completely, he turned back to glance at her one last time. "Good night, Blythe."

"Good night, Finn." With that, he shut the door and she heard his heavy footsteps as he walked away from her.

She slipped out of her clothes carefully, pulling his shirt over her head. It smelled like him. This entire room smelled just like his metallic cologne. She laid down in his bed, enjoying the scent surrounding every inch of her. She wasn't sure what it was about this man that had her so enraptured—perhaps the mystery, perhaps that he'd been so kind on a day that she'd really needed kindness—either way, the thoughts she was having about him would've had Aunt Patty clutching her pearls.

She turned off the lamp on his bedside table, listening to the fan above her whirling around, and tried to fall asleep. Outside, she could hear sirens, horns, and people laughing. *The sounds of New York City.* It was incredibly noisy. She rolled over, wrapping her head in a pillow. She'd certainly have to get used to this.

Then again, Aunt Patty's home wasn't going to be this noisy...was it? And she'd only be at Finn's for the night. So, this noise was only temporary.

After a few minutes of tossing and turning and wishing desperately for her phone and earphones to drown out the thoughts of the mile-long to-do list she now had to complete—a trip to the nearest DMV at the top of that list—she threw the covers off her legs and walked from the room. She didn't want to think of all the misfortune the robber had cost her: the bank card she'd need to replace, the only family photos she owned now in the hands of a stranger; she just wanted to sleep.

He was sitting on the couch, staring at a blank TV. He looked up, surprised to see her. "Need something?" he asked.

"I...I can't sleep," she said, bumping one knee into the other awkwardly.

He seemed to understand, patting the seat next to him. It was an invitation. She took him up on his offer without much coaxing, sliding onto the couch next to him and watching as he picked up the remote. "Any preferences?" he asked.

She shook her head, leaning over onto his chest without hesitation. He was right, without pillows this couch certainly wasn't comfortable. He didn't seem to mind her weight, scooting further down into the couch in what seemed like an attempt to make her more relaxed.

She could hear his heart racing in his chest, and she wondered if he could hear hers. His hand stroked her arm carefully, causing the hair on her arms to raise.

It had been so long since she'd touched anyone else… as painful as that was to admit. A year. A year since her parents died and she dumped her high school boyfriend. A year since her life effectively stopped.

He flipped through the channels casually, though she was pretty sure he wasn't actually paying attention to what was on. She closed her eyes for a split second, focusing on his heartbeat and finally allowing herself to succumb to her exhaustion.

Next thing she knew, she woke up.

CHAPTER THREE

She opened her eyes in a strange place. It took awhile for her vision to adjust to the light streaming into the window and then for her brain to catch up.

"Sorry," a voice whispered from underneath her. They were lying on a couch in an apartment she didn't immediately recognize. She looked over, staring at Finn with what she was sure was a strange expression. "I didn't mean to wake you...I just really need to pee." He lifted her head from his chest, darting across the apartment in a hurry.

She rubbed the sleep from her eyes, the past day's events coming back to her. She hadn't slept so well in over a year. Apparently, the city's sounds grew on her faster than she'd ever imagined.

When he reappeared, his messy hair was combed and his lips were red. He'd brushed his teeth—something she desperately needed to do.

She escaped from the room, staring at his toothbrush for a moment and considering the insane possibility of using it, before she held out her finger under the tube and ran it quickly through her mouth. She pinched her cheeks —something she'd seen her mother do when she wanted to impress someone, ran a hand through her dark brown hair, and shrugged. It was the best it was going to get, she supposed.

When she walked from the room, Finn had started making coffee. He had a mug sitting out for her but didn't say anything as she walked past it. She had never liked coffee, but if he offered, she would accept the cup. It was the polite thing to do. Besides, load it up with cream and sugar and it was practically dessert.

She slid onto the barstool. "So," she said, clearing her throat. "Good morning, I guess."

He smiled from behind his mug. "Good morning." She looked away, but when she looked back, his eyes were still locked on her as if in awe. As he noticed her meeting his stare, he looked down.

Heat rose to her cheeks. "What do you have planned for the day?" she asked.

He glanced at the clock. "I have to be at work soon," he said, his eyes studying hers.

I've overstayed my welcome. It hit her quickly, and she stood even quicker, nearly knocking over the stool. "I'm so sorry. I should be going."

He placed the mug down. "I didn't mean you had to leave."

"No, honestly, you've done way too much for me as it is. I'll call my aunt from the…"

He slid his phone across the counter. "You can use my phone. But you're welcome to stay. Honestly, you are. I'll be home later tonight, but you can make yourself at home. Or head out and take care of whatever you need to. As long as you need it, the bed...or *couch,* since that seems to be your preference, is yours. Trust me, I've been at the point of crashing on couches and staying with people who truly don't want me there."

She nodded. "Thank you, but I couldn't."

He shrugged, pushing the phone further toward her until she took it. "Well, the offer stands either way. I need to get a shower." He stared at her for a moment, and she was sure he wanted to say something else, but he didn't. Instead, he turned to walk down the hallway and she watched him disappear, her throat dry and heart strangely empty.

She dialed her aunt's number, listening as it rang and rang. When she didn't answer, Blythe left a message, explaining to her exactly where she'd be and that she didn't have a phone so she wouldn't be able to reach her. She laid the phone back on the counter, watching the blank screen as she hoped her aunt would call her back.

After a few minutes, Blythe heard the water from his shower shut off, and as much as she wanted to, she couldn't move. The bathroom door opened, and she watched a cloud of steam waft down the hallway. After a few moments, she heard his padded footsteps coming her way.

When she saw him she gasped without meaning to. His black towel was wrapped tightly around his tan waist, revealing a soaking wet six-pack of abs she hadn't been expecting. His messy, brown hair was wet and hanging down around his chin, and his eyes widened when he saw her.

"Sorry, I didn't think you'd still be here," he said simply.

"I...shouldn't be," she said honestly. "My...I was... waiting for my aunt to call back." Suddenly, her words were taking forever to form and her eyes couldn't be pulled from his skin.

He nodded but didn't say anything.

"Anyway, I really should be going. I left her a message about where to find me." She turned, bumping into the stool and sending it flying this time. They both moved to grab it, and their skin touched, lightning shooting through her. He tucked a piece of his dark hair behind his ear as she spun around to face him. "S-sorry," she said.

"Blythe," he said, her name on his tongue sending shivers down her spine. "You're fine. Stop apologizing."

She nodded, her eyes studying his hauntingly dark stare. "O-okay. Sorry."

He closed his eyes for a half-second, a small smile on his lips. When he opened them, he asked, "Are you sure you don't want to stay?"

She shook her head, though every fiber of her being was screaming *yes*, and spit out the word, "No." She bit her lip. "I shouldn't. I can't thank you enough for all you've already done for me."

He touched her arm, and a squeal nearly escaped her chest but she managed to rein it in. Did she do to him what he did to her? It wasn't possible. This was the product of a small-town, sheltered girl finally meeting someone, *anyone,* new. That had to be it. "Like I said, the offer stands. I get off at seven. I'll be here. Anytime."

She smiled nervously. "Thank you, Finn."

Was it her imagination, or had she seen his eyes grow dark with desire as she spoke his name? She closed her eyes, literally shaking away the thought and stepping back. She couldn't be here, or she was going to end up making a fool of herself. He didn't come after her as she grabbed her clothes from the floor and hurried out of the apartment, calling out a quick, "Thank you again," over her shoulder.

CHAPTER FOUR

ONE MONTH LATER

Blythe hurried back into the kitchen, trying to catch her breath in between trays of food. She was surprised to see a guest with his head in the large, double-doored, stainless steel fridge.

"Looking for something in particular?" she asked. It was unusual to find a guest in the kitchen during a catered event. In fact, it was her entire job to make sure guests never had to step foot in the kitchen, so as she watched him turn around with a mouthful of food, his pale skin turning pink, she wasn't sure whether to feel disappointment or pleasure. At least it looked like he was enjoying the food.

"Oh, hey," he said, trying to cover his still-full mouth and swallow quickly. Once his mouth was empty, he let out a sigh. "You caught me."

She smirked. "It's okay…can I get something for you?"

"Honestly, if you can just forget that you saw me,

that'd be great," he said, leaning across the marble island with a cocky grin.

"Right," she said, unsure of how to take his request. "Okay, sure." She picked up a tray of food, turning to walk back out into the study where a swarm of guests would be waiting for the next round. "Consider yourself forgotten."

"Wait," he said, pausing for her to turn around before he spoke again, "what's your name?"

She shook her head, caught off guard by the question. "Um, I'm Blythe."

"Blythe," he said, smiling as he said the word. "I like that."

She nodded. "My mother would've been happy to hear that." There was that pang of grief again at the mere mention of her mother.

He laughed. "I'm Asher." His hand extended out for hers, and she balanced the tray with one hand to reach back. He held onto her for longer than necessary, but the pounding in her chest told her that didn't matter. "Do... uh, do you want to get out of here?"

She furrowed her brow, motioning toward the tray of food. "I'm kind of working."

He scowled. "Oh, come on, I'll pay you double whatever they're paying you. Let's slip out and go grab a drink. This party is...stuffy, isn't it?"

She bit her lip, contemplating it only for a moment. "I'm sorry, I can't."

He looked disappointed, though he recovered quickly. "Okay, fine. I guess I can stick around until you're done. Just...if anyone asks, you haven't seen me."

"You're just going to stay in here?" she asked.

He tossed a torte in his mouth from her tray. "Yep," he said, popping the p.

"But why? If you hate this party so much, why are you even here?"

"It's...well, this is an old-friend-of-the-family thing. And I'm supposed to be here because of family obligations, yada yada yada. Truth be told, I'm bored to tears." He fidgeted with his tie as if it were suddenly choking him. "This isn't typically my scene."

"What is your scene, then?" she asked.

He narrowed his eyes at her. "Wouldn't you like to know?" he said cockily. "So, anyway, you down to be my lookout?"

She smiled, easily charmed by his warm smile and dark eyes. "Sure, I'll do what I can."

"Thanks," he said. "And remember," he said as she opened the door, "you never saw me."

"You who?" she asked, closing the door behind her as she re-entered the study, greeted quickly by hungry guests.

TWO HOURS LATER, the party was over and Blythe was exhausted and wanted to get home to her aunt's. After the dishes had been washed and she collected her check and loaded up the company van, she was surprised to see Asher appear behind her in the alley where she'd parked. He hadn't been in the kitchen when she returned, so she assumed he'd gotten bored with the party and ditched, but she was relieved to see that wasn't the case.

"Well, glad that's over," he said, leaning one arm against her van as she leaned back against it. She jingled the keys in her hand.

"It must've been so exhausting for you," she teased.

He chuckled, patting his stomach. "It was a lot of work. So, where to next?"

She shrugged. "I have to take the van back to the shop, but after that, I guess we can hang out for a little while."

His eyes were suddenly filled with heat, and she felt flushed. "Well, I like the sound of that," he said, his voice a low growl. "Come on," he cleared his throat, "the night is young."

She climbed into the car, watching as he sank into the passenger's seat. She wasn't technically allowed to have non-employees in the van with her, but what was she going to do?

She pulled out of the alley and headed into traffic. The small, downtown shop that housed her employer's catering business was just a few blocks away, and within minutes she was dropping off the empty dishes and the check. She was thankful no one was in the building, one of the perks of working most of the late shifts.

She walked back out of the building, staring at him as he stood by a parking meter. He'd loosened his tie and rolled up his shirt sleeves, looking entirely more comfortable than before.

He grinned at her, his smile sending blood to her cheeks. "You ready?"

"Where to?"

He pointed straight ahead at a dimly lit restaurant with a valet standing out front. "I thought you could use some food. You must be exhausted. Have you ever tried Evan's?"

"I haven't," she answered, shaking her head. "Is it any good?"

A scoff escaped his throat, as if that were an absurd question. "It's only the best seafood on the East Coast."

She stared at the large entranceway. "It...looks busy. Are you sure we can even get in?"

"The owner's a friend," he said, waving her toward him as they hurried across the street. He walked past the valet without a word, one arm around her, and led her into the restaurant. "Table for two. Asher Grace," he said, holding up two fingers.

The maître d' nodded, stepping away from the stand for a moment and reappearing with two menus. He held out an arm, allowing them past the open door and further into the restaurant. Their table was near the back, and though the restaurant was lit with lights above their tables, there was a candle in the middle to add to the ambiance.

When the waiter approached the table, Asher asked if they could have a minute to look over the menu.

He opened hers for her, handing it over. "What do you like?"

"Oh," she said, looking over the menu with an over-whelming sense of choices. "Um, maybe salmon? I've not eaten a lot of seafood."

"Salmon's a great choice," he said, smiling at her. "Do you like fish? I guess I should've asked that first. We can go somewhere else if you prefer...or they have chicken—"

"No," she said. "I do like fish, I'm just still getting used to all the options New York has."

He nodded, sliding his chair around so he was sitting beside her rather than across from her. He leaned in, flipping the pages of her menu. "Here, they have a sampler. You can try everything they serve. Smaller portions, of course, but then you'll get a feel for what you truly like so you'll know next time we're here."

"Next time?" she asked, incredibly aware of how close he was.

"Yeah," he told her, turning his head to face her. "At least, *I hope* there'll be a next time."

She brushed a piece of hair from her face. "I hope so, too," she said quietly, welcoming the warm smile that grew on his lips. She couldn't deny he was handsome. His perfectly proportioned face, short pompadour hair, and whitened teeth would make him the perfect candidate for a Calvin Klein photoshoot. And she had him all to herself for the evening.

Granted, she couldn't have guessed what made him interested in her. She was still dressed in her server's uniform, reeking of food, with very little makeup on, and her brown hair tossed back into a clip. She wasn't exactly the picture of beauty on a good day, but today was far from good.

"So, what do you say?" he asked. "Do you want to try it all?"

"It's super expensive," she said, her eyes widening as she noticed the price.

"Don't worry about that," he said, patting her hand and taking the menu from her. "Whatever you want tonight... it's yours."

WHEN THE DINNER WAS DONE, Asher paid their tab and led her out the door. Her belly was full of lobster—her new favorite—and salmon, plus a cheesy biscuit that was to die for.

"You good?" he asked, watching her as she rubbed her belly in a trance-like state.

She moved her hand from her stomach instantly, letting out a laugh. "Sorry. Yeah, I'm good. That was…amazing."

He smiled. "I'm glad you liked it. I'll tell my friend."

"I can't believe someone your age owns a restaurant like that."

"How old do you think I am?" he asked.

She squinted her eyes at him. "Not much older than me. I'd say…early twenties?"

He nodded. "I'm twenty-seven. Evan's twenty-eight. What about you?"

"Twenty-two," she said simply. "And I have nothing in my life figured out, in case you were wondering. Certainly not to the point that I could open up a restaurant in New York City. That's…incredible." He watched her in amazement, and she suddenly realized how crazy she must sound. "Sorry. I just…I'm impressed."

"No need to apologize, though I do hope Evan's not trying to steal my girl," he said, reaching for her hand.

"Oh, I'm *your* girl now?"

"For tonight, you are," he said, pulling her to walk in the opposite direction. "And maybe tomorrow, too."

"Well, I'm sorry for talking so much about Evan," she

said softly, noting the playful look on his face. He was teasing, but she honestly couldn't blame him if he were upset. Who wanted to go on a date and have their date dote on someone else the whole time? "So, what do you do, Asher?"

"I'm afraid it's not nearly so impressive," he told her. "I'm in advertising. Which, I know, sounds cool, but honestly it's just paper pushing all day."

She squeezed his hand. "That's *very* cool."

He glanced at her, his eyebrows raised and he let out a sarcastic laugh. "Thanks, Mom," he joked. He looked back ahead of them. "No, it's pretty alright, ya know? I mean, it pays the bills and it can be kind of fun."

She nodded. "Better than catering, right?"

"No wonder you were so impressed by the restaurant. You must love to cook," he said, as if that were just dawning on him.

"I love to bake," she corrected. "But, this will do for now. Truth be told, I have no idea what I want to do long term, but the company was hiring and I just went for it. I'm new to the city, so I needed something to keep the bills paid while I look for a new place and try to get my life somewhat together."

"Where are you from?" he asked.

"Texas."

"Ahh," he said, wagging a finger at her. "I knew that was a Southern accent."

She feigned a pout. "And I was trying so hard to hide it."

He chuckled. "How long have you been in New York?"

"Not long," she said.

"Are you planning to stay?"

"Funny enough, I like it here. I never pictured myself as a city girl, and I'm still not entirely convinced, but there's something freeing about being here, isn't there? Like…I feel so invisible. It's kind of exciting."

He stopped, pulling her under the awning of a building. "It's exciting to be invisible?" he asked, turning her so that she faced him.

She nodded, pressing her lips together. "Kind of. Does that sound crazy? I'm from a small town and, well, everyone knows you there. Going to Wal-Mart without makeup on is like…front page news. Everyone knows everything you do, and it's suffocating. Sometimes I just want to be able to live my life without people judging me, ya know?"

He raised an eyebrow when she huffed out a final breath. "What's a Wal-Mart?" he asked.

She released an exasperated laugh, her laughter releasing her from the pressure she'd been under for so long. For a moment, she couldn't seem to contain herself, which only made him laugh along. Whatever they were laughing at, it wasn't truly as funny as the fact that they couldn't seem to contain their laughter.

After a moment, she finally calmed down, patting his chest with her palm. "You are such a city boy."

"Born and raised," he told her. "So, I wouldn't know much about small towns, but I know a lot about trying to live your life without judgement. I think that's something everyone wants, no matter their zip code."

"Maybe so…" she said, trailing off.

"So, how about we go up to my place and make some

decisions that we could easily be judged for tomorrow?" he asked, running a finger along her arm.

"I…um." She bit her lip. She hadn't slept with a man since she broke up with Danny, and as much as she was attracted to Asher, she couldn't deny the fact that sleeping with someone new was terrifying. And she wished she'd had more preparation.

"You don't have to if you don't want to," he assured her, his voice low. His expression was sincere as he spoke again. "I just don't want this night to be over."

"You live here?" she asked, staring at the doorman just beyond the door. He was giving them complete privacy, not bothering to turn his head in their direction at all. All around them, people were walking past, carrying on conversations that were entirely their own. No one noticed them. No one paid them any attention. *Invisible.* It felt so good.

Who cared what she did? Who cared if she slept with a man that was practically a stranger? Every choice she made was entirely her own. She'd never known that kind of freedom.

"I do," he told her.

"Okay," she said finally, her decision made.

"Okay?" he asked, his lips grazing hers cautiously.

She opened her mouth, allowing the kiss to happen as it sent chills down her spine. When he pulled away, his eyes were drunk with desire and she said the word that she'd been dying to say. "Okay." For the first time in her life, making a decision based solely on what she wanted… was *okay*.

CHAPTER FIVE

Blythe woke up to the feeling of a kiss being placed on her forehead. The previous night was a blur of kisses and tangled sheets, and she wasn't sure how to feel about her impulsiveness with someone who was basically a stranger. She opened her eyes slowly, staring at the handsome sight across the pillow from her. He was propped up on his elbow, brushing a piece of hair from her eyes.

"Good morning," he said, his voice throaty from sleep. He traced a finger across her arm lovingly.

"Good morning," she said happily, burying her face in the pillow. "What time is it?" she asked.

"Almost ten," he told her. "I would've let you sleep, but your phone has been going off."

She rolled over, checking the message on her screen. "It's my boss." She groaned, pulling the blanket up to cover her bare breasts as she moved the phone toward her. "Giving me the address for my shift tonight."

He nodded. "Did you sleep well?"

"I did, actually."

"Why do you sound surprised?" He raised a brow, staring at her with his honey-brown eyes.

"Because I don't usually sleep well with so much noise going on outside. I've only actually slept *in* New York City one other time, and it took me forever to fall asleep."

"Guess I wore you out then, huh?" he teased, kissing her square on the lips. She welcomed his kiss, despite the morning breath she knew she must have, feeling his body warm against hers as he slid over toward her. And what a nice body it was—chiseled and toned in all the right areas, yet not overly buff. It was obvious he took pride in himself, something Blythe had always found attractive. She was used to hardworking farmers, so six-pack abs and muscled arms tended to be her weakness.

He surprised her by pulling away. "Do you want breakfast?" he asked.

She rubbed her lips where his mouth had been. "Uh, sure," she said. "I thought you were going for round two." She winked.

He kissed her lips again. "Can't use up all my strength for later, now can I?"

"Later? What's later?" she asked as he climbed out of bed and slid on his boxers, giving her quite a show as she didn't look away.

"I'm taking you to a dinner party."

"A dinner party?" she asked. "For what?"

"It's a work thing," he said. "You'll have to blow off *your* work, though." He leaned back down over the bed, trailing a kiss from her neck to her chest. "But I promise to make it worth your while."

She sucked in a breath, ignoring what he'd said as his tongue explored her skin. When he pulled away, she sat up, throwing her shirt over her shoulders and buttoning it without the bra. She pulled on her jeans afterward. "I don't know if I can miss work. I'm brand new."

"Just tell them you're sick. I'll write them a stellar review from the party last night. And…if they fire you, I'll find you a new job."

"You can't just do that," she argued, though there was little fight left to her voice.

"And why not?" he asked, reaching for her hand as she walked around to his side of the bed.

"Because…the world doesn't work that way. You can't have whatever you want just because you say so."

He winked. "I got you, didn't I?"

AFTER BREAKFAST, Asher ordered clothes for her and had them delivered within an hour. The man was obviously used to getting whatever he wanted. She sent a quick text to her boss, explaining that she'd woken up sick, and followed Asher out the door without a second thought.

The clothes he'd picked out fit well, and she felt much more comfortable than she had the night before in her uniform. He led her down the stairs of his apartment building, past the doorman from last night with a slight nod of acknowledgement, and onto the busy street. That was another thing Blythe had yet to get used to. No matter where you were or what time it was, New York was always busy. There were people everywhere all the time. She guessed she'd known it would be the case, but she hadn't understood the magnitude of its busyness until she arrived. It was breathtaking the amount of people there were in the city, and in a way, it gave her the room she needed to breathe. No one was there to notice that she was outside with a man when she'd just called into work. No one would be reporting said news to her aunt or her boss because no one knew her there. Say what you will about large cities, but that alone was enough to keep her there.

"Where are we going?" she asked loudly, as he pulled her across the busy street at a near-run.

"We have to get you something to wear, don't we?"

"What do you call what I have on?" she asked, when they reached the other side of the street and she looked down at her outfit.

"Yes, well, those are great for right now, but tonight is black tie."

She gasped. It all sounded so fancy. "Asher, I can't keep letting you spend so much money on me. I'm starting to feel bad."

He rolled his eyes playfully. "I want to do it or I wouldn't be, so don't worry about it."

"Are you sure?" she asked. "I mean, I have a little bit of money. I could help some."

"This party is for me. When you take me to a fancy dinner party, you can pay for my tux, okay? Deal?"

She stared at him, at the kindness behind his eyes that she hadn't noticed before, the dimple in his chin, and the way he stared at her with such interest. He made her feel like the only girl on the crowded street, and that was something she'd never felt before. In Darlington, she was a choice only because the choices were so limited. In New York, the choices were endless, yet Asher had chosen her.

"Deal," she agreed, taking his hand as he held it out again. If she had the option, she would've stayed right there in his grip, and in his eye line, for as long as she possibly could.

A few doors down, Asher pulled her into a dress shop. "This place is good. A few of the women I work with have ordered from here before. Take a look around." He held out an arm. "Let me know what you like."

Somehow he seemed to make even the most innocent of sentences provocative. "Okay," she said, staring around. She walked toward a mannequin dressed in a simple, black dress, running her fingers over the fabric. She had no idea what size she would need—most of her dresses were sized with letters, not numbers.

"Oh, no." A voice came from her side. She looked up to see a perky saleswoman with stark black hair approaching her. "That dress isn't right for you," she said, her voice polite though her words stung. "Pretty brown hair with just a perfect hint of red like you've got—we need a fiery dress to match a fiery woman." She winked at her, taking her arm and leading her across the room. She cast a friendly glance over her shoulder toward Asher, making Blythe wonder if they knew each other.

"Okay," Blythe said hesitantly. Asher took a seat in an oversized, white chair, seeming to be enjoying the view as the woman led her toward a mannequin wearing a floor-length red gown. The neckline was cut close to where she assumed her belly button would land; it had her blushing at the mere thought of wearing it. Her mother would've had a fit.

"How about this one?" the woman asked. "With a red lip, too, this would really help you to stand out."

"Oh, I don't know..." Blythe said softly, running her fingers over the fabric. It was a beautiful dress, there was no denying that. Whoever wore it would certainly have all the attention on her, but did she want that? She'd never been comfortable with being the center of attention.

"Would you like to try it on?" she offered. "Trust me, you and this dress..." She made an 'okay' symbol with her forefinger and thumb. "He won't know what hit him."

Blythe smiled, looking back over her shoulder to where Asher was watching and waiting. He smiled at her, sending warmth throughout her body. "Okay," she said before she allowed herself to second-guess it. "I'll try it on."

"Perfect," the sales woman squealed. "Now, let me look at you." She placed a fist under her chin as her eyes trailed over Blythe's body. "You're...what? A size twelve, maybe?"

"Maybe," Blythe said nervously. "I don't really know."

"No problem," the woman assured her. "Here." She grabbed two dresses from the rack. "We'll try a twelve and a ten, and if these don't work, we'll come back for more." With that, she whisked her away toward a dressing room, and Blythe tried to enjoy the morning in whoever's life she'd somehow ended up, while it lasted.

WHEN BLYTHE WALKED out of the dressing room, sucked

into the size twelve, she looked around the room for him. At first, she didn't see him, surprised that he'd left the chair. Had this all been a prank? Was he trying to ditch her?

For just that moment, her heart lurched and she felt sure she was going to be sick. Within a minute, she laid eyes on him. He was standing at the opposite side of the room, talking with one of the saleswomen. When he saw her, his expression grew ashen and he walked away from the woman quickly, his eyes locked on her.

"Whoa," he said as he grew near.

She looked down over the red fabric, trying to pretend she didn't feel like a movie star on the red carpet. It was the most beautiful piece of clothing she'd ever worn. "You like it?" she asked, not meeting his eye.

He cleared his throat. "It's...um...it's—"

"I can try on something else," she said quickly.

"It's perfect," he told her, reaching down to take her hand. "You look beautiful."

She looked up at him then, her heart racing. In the middle of the store, surrounded by random onlookers, he leaned toward her, unaware of or simply unfazed by the people that would see them. His lips met hers, one hand cupping her scalp as she melted into his kiss. He was warm and familiar, a kiss she hadn't known she could miss so much in the half hour since she'd last experienced it.

When he pulled away, he looked at the saleswoman over Blythe's shoulder. Blythe ran a finger over her lips as she heard him speak. "We'll take it."

THAT EVENING, Blythe opened the bedroom door and walked out to the living room where Asher was waiting. He stood immediately upon seeing her. "You look... incredible," he told her. She'd chosen to wear her hair clipped to one side with curls throughout, a style she'd seen in some of her favorite magazines but never attempted herself. So, she was glad when he seemed to like it. He twirled his finger through the tendril of hair she'd left out near her ear. "Red is definitely your color."

"Thank you," she said, thankful he felt that way as she knew her cheeks must be growing redder by the minute. "Everything seems to be your color."

He smiled, letting out a soft laugh as he buttoned the black suit jacket he was wearing. Underneath, he'd chosen a simple black tie and white shirt. He was breathtaking no matter what he wore, but seeing him in a tux made it hard to take her eyes off of him.

He ran a quick hand over his messy-on-purpose blond hair and bent his arm at his waist, waiting for her to run her arm through the opening. "You ready?"

She slid her arm through his, walking out the door with a racing heart. She couldn't stop smiling, and it was starting to hurt her cheeks.

When they climbed into the cab, he rubbed a finger over his jaw. "So, are you glad you skipped work tonight?"

"This is definitely more fun," she agreed. "Thank you... for inviting me."

"I'm glad you could come," he told her, pressing his lips into her head. "They're going to love you."

"Are you sure?" she asked. "I've never been to a fancy New York party. I'm not sure I'll fit in."

"Trust me, you'll do fine. I'll be right here the whole time. Just stick with me, and I'll have you turned into the life of the party in no time." She shook her head, not sure she believed him but thankful for the encouragement. "Besides," he told her, "it'll be nice to have some fresh blood at these parties. It's usually the same old boring wives and girlfriends of my coworkers. A new face will liven things up." He traced a finger over her shoulder. "The guys are going to be so jealous I'm going home with the most beautiful girl at the party."

She scoffed, rolling her eyes, but she couldn't deny that he knew all the right things to say. She leaned in as he did, feeling their lips collide again.

"I'm so glad I met you," she said when they separated.

"At least something good came from that terrible party," he agreed.

"I mean it," she told him. "I know we just met, but… you make me really happy."

He squeezed her hand, looking out the window as they rounded the corner. "We're here," he told her. "Come on, beautiful." Asher stepped from the cab, handing over a stack of bills to the driver with a quick thanks, and holding out his hand to help Blythe.

She stepped out, looking up at the tall skyscraper that was in front of them. "This is where you work?" she asked.

He nodded, pointing up toward the building. "Sixteenth floor."

"I'm afraid of heights," she admitted. "I couldn't get anything done if I were up that high."

He sucked in a breath. "Well, that might be a problem. The party is on the roof."

"What?" she asked as he pulled her inside past two doormen and into an elevator. "I don't know if I can be up that high."

"I'll protect you," he said. "I promise you'll be fine. The ledges are taller than we are. Short of you planning to jump, there's no chance you'll fall."

She nodded, feeling only slightly better as they rode to the top. When the elevator doors opened, she gasped. It was a party like she'd only seen in the movies. Everyone was dressed up, waiters swarmed with cocktails and appetizers, and the partygoers looked incredibly happy. And why shouldn't they be? They were gorgeous. Each and every one of them looked as though they could've stepped straight out of the pages of a magazine.

"Breathe," Asher warned, and she realized she'd been holding her breath. She let it out.

"Sorry," she whispered.

He wrapped an arm around her waist, pulling her closer as they made their way through the party. She couldn't help but notice that a few eyes had started to drift toward them—more specifically, her—and she heard his words in her head again. *New blood.*

An older couple approached them first, the man's bald head held a shining reflection from the lights around the edges of the building. "Asher," the man said, reaching out his hand.

Asher shook the man's hand warmly, moving his hand

from Blythe's waist to touch his arm. "Mr. O'Connor, sir, I'd like to introduce you to my date, Blythe."

"Blythe," the man said politely. "It's a pleasure to meet you." He looked at Asher with raised eyebrows, and for a moment Blythe thought he was going to compliment her. "Did you see we snagged the Deluthe account?"

Asher let out a confident laugh. "I did."

"Well done, m'boy," Mr. O'Connor said, patting his shoulder. "Elderman will be getting a call Monday morning, you can bet on that." He wagged a finger in the air. "Well, I'll leave you to it. I've got to catch up with Chad and see if he's heard anything about the Miracle account. Nice to meet you again, Bright." With that, he offered Blythe a quick handshake and disappeared.

"Sorry about that," Asher said. "He's never been very good with names."

"Is that your boss?" she asked.

He nodded, grabbing two glasses of champagne from a passing waiter and handing one to Blythe. "Thank you," she told the waiter, tapping her glass against Asher's. "It's weird being here and not being one of them."

"Well, get used to it," he told her, his eyes burning into hers.

"I don't know if I could ever get used to this," she told him honestly, looking around the crowded party.

"Come on, you attend fancy parties all the time."

"It's not exactly attending, and honestly, no. I attend parties like the one I met you at...mostly in houses, and though they're nice, they're nothing like this."

"Well, I know it looks fancy, but honestly, it's mostly just about impressing our clients. If it were up to most of the guys here, we'd all be at a sports bar with a bottle of beer." He smirked, waving as they passed a few of his colleagues. He introduced Blythe to a few more men as they hurried past, making their way to a far corner of the roof.

"Your job must be so fun," she mused, wrapping one arm around her middle to protect herself from the cool breeze.

"It can be," he admitted. "But it can also be super stressful." He nudged her hip. "Which is why I'm thankful I ran into you."

She looked up at him, shocked by his words. "You are?"

"Yeah. I mean, you're so low key, Blythe. It's kind of refreshing. New York girls are...stressful and dramatic and...honestly, I've never met anyone like you."

She offered a small smile. "I'm nothing special," she drawled.

"You are," he told her, lifting her chin so she would look at him when she looked away. "You are special." With that, his lips met hers and the party faded away. She lifted one arm, draping it over his shoulder as his arms went around her waist. She'd never felt more special in her life.

CHAPTER SIX

"Have a good night, Cathy," Blythe called to her coworker as she exited the building. She'd worked two parties back to back, and Blythe was thankful when Cathy offered to clean everything up so she could go home and catch some sleep. What she really wanted was to get out of her shoes—she was exhausted, and her feet were on fire.

She stuck a few of her tips into her back pocket—mostly ones—but held onto a twenty as she spied a coffee cart up ahead. She needed something to help her stay awake on the cab ride to the suburbs. She approached the young man, holding out the bill. "Double shot Americano please." Who cared that she hated coffee? If she couldn't stay awake, she wasn't sure what might happen. Her luck, she'd end up a state away with a sky-high cab bill.

He took the cash, slipping it in his pocket and pouring her a glass. She stared at the sign on his cart, letting her know he accepted PayPal and Venmo. When he handed her the drink, she thanked him and turned around, ready to walk away when something caught her eye. She froze in her spot, despite the agitated people in line behind her just waiting for their turn to order.

She stared through the glass of the restaurant, the glare on the windows making it hard to tell if she was seeing what she thought she was. She swallowed, taking a step forward and placing one hand over her brow to shield her eyes from the light. Without conscious thought, she found herself headed into the restaurant.

"Asher?" she said as she approached his table. The brunette with the pompadour turned, confirming her fears.

He was sitting at a small table across from a woman with strawberry-blonde hair and a dark tan. When she smiled, her teeth were almost too white.

"Blythe? What are you doing here?" he asked, staring up at her with a look of confusion.

"Better question…what are *you* doing here?" she asked, gesturing toward his date. She was exhausted, which was only aiding her irritability. Normally she would've been much more reserved; she rarely chose to start a conflict, but she couldn't hold it in.

"I'm…on a date," he said slowly. "This is Bianca."

"Hi—" Bianca started to say, waving her fingers pleasantly.

"Seriously? A date?" She took a breath, nodding her head slowly. "Okay." Turning away from him as tears formed in her eyes, she walked out of the restaurant in a hurry. She couldn't let him see her cry. Granted, they'd only been seeing each other for a few weeks, but it hurt nonetheless. She'd truly grown to like him.

"Blythe, wait," he called, grabbing her arm as she exited the restaurant.

She spun around to face him. "What, Asher?"

"What are you doing here?" he asked. "Are you mad?"

"Am I mad? Of course, I'm mad! You're cheating on me!" she squealed.

"Cheating on you?" He furrowed his brow, putting a hand to his chest. "Wait a second, Blythe, I'm not...I'm not *cheating* on you. We aren't exclusive." He said the words slowly, surprising her with how blunt he was being.

"We aren't?" she asked, staring into her drink. How could she have been so stupid? She felt like a child who'd been scolded.

"I mean, we never had that talk. I just assumed we were on the same page. Look, I like you a lot and I want to keep seeing you. But I can't commit to anything serious right now. I'm sorry if you misunderstood. That wasn't my intention." He used his thumb to brush away a stray tear from her cheek, leaning down to look at her. "I'm really sorry, Blythe."

She nodded. "I'm sorry, too. I guess I should've known. I just...I don't know. I really like you."

"I really like you, too," he said, stroking her cheek. "I do. I'd like to see you again. But only if you're okay with this."

"This? As in you seeing other people?"

"As in both of us seeing other people," he corrected. "You're new to the city. You need to explore and try new things. I'm nowhere near ready to settle down yet, and you shouldn't be either. It doesn't mean I don't want to be with you, it just means I'm not sure I want to be with anyone just yet. I mean, I'm twenty-seven years old." He shrugged, keeping his voice light.

She wanted desperately to accept what he was saying, but she wasn't sure she could. She felt tricked, even though realistically she knew that wasn't the case. She'd believed Asher wanted to be with her and only her, but that belief was formulated only in her mind rather than being based on anything he'd actually told her. In Darlington, twenty-seven typically meant you were settled down, married, and raising two children. But New York was different. People settled down later here. She'd seen that. She knew that. And yet somehow, in her heart, she still hoped for what she'd always known. She wanted to love and to be loved. Exclusively.

"I don't know if I can do that," she admitted, biting her lip.

His gaze fell to the ground and he removed his hand from her cheek. "Okay," he said. "I can respect that." He leaned forward, kissing her forehead. "If you change your mind, you know how to find me."

She nodded, not meeting his gaze.

"It was really nice getting to know you, Blythe," he said. With that, he disappeared back into the restaurant, and she was left alone with her racing thoughts.

She wandered the streets, sipping her coffee and trying to determine her next move. If she went home still upset, her aunt would surely have things to say about her *lifestyle*. She wasn't in a place to handle that.

As she took the last drink from her cup, noticing the sky had grown dark as she wandered around for nearly two hours, she tossed the paper cup into a nearby trashcan and stepped out onto the curb to wave down a cab. When she looked up, she gasped, surprised to find the building in front of her was a familiar one.

Without thinking too much about it, she hurried into the building and up the stairs. This was crazy. What she was doing was certifiably insane, and yet, with every step, she felt a bit more safe. A bit less heartbroken. As she reached his floor, she approached his door with her fist raised.

Knock, knock, knock. Why hadn't she come here sooner? Why had she stayed away from the one person who'd protected her when she'd stepped into the city for the first time? She regretted it now, and she wondered what he would say to her. Would he blame her for waiting so long? Would he even remember her? Surely he'd met loads of people since then.

As the door swung open, she smiled at the surprised face awaiting her. He looked the same, his scraggly brown hair hanging down past his ears, dark brown eyes staring into hers. He was shirtless with a pair of unbuttoned jeans around his waist.

"Bly—"

"Fin—"

They greeted each other at the same time, a small laugh escaping her throat. He remembered her. "Can I come in?" she asked boldly, expecting him to open the door wider.

"Who is it?" a voice called from just behind him. A woman's voice. He opened the door a bit more, leaning his head against the wood, and Blythe stared at a young, red-headed woman with a blue T-shirt and no bottoms on. She was dressed in Finn's clothes.

"Oh," Blythe said, because no words seemed to fit.

"What are you doing here?" Finn asked, and she stared at him blankly because the truth was, she had no idea.

CHAPTER SEVEN

"What are you doing here?" he repeated, staring at her with a strange expression. He looked as confused as she felt. What *was* she doing there? The truth was, she'd longed to be at the last place she felt truly safe...which, as it turned out, was Finn's apartment. But why was that true? He was basically a stranger, after all.

He was still waiting for an answer and the air around them was growing thicker with tension, so she backed away, blinking herself out of the trance and clearing her throat. "I'm so sorry." She turned to walk away from the apartment when she heard him speak.

"Blythe?" he called her name, and she spun back around to face him as if pulled by magnets.

"Yes?" she asked, her voice wavering slightly.

"Do you need me?" he asked, studying her expression with his head cocked to the side.

She shook her head, but her eyes filled with sudden, betraying tears. Without another word, Finn looked behind him. "I'm sorry," he apologized to the woman who was struggling to get her pants back on. "We're going to have to take a raincheck."

"A raincheck?" she asked, disdain clearly in her voice. "You're kidding, right?"

"Not really," he said, his voice firm. "You need to leave."

The woman scoffed, grabbing her clothes from the floor and casting an angry look his way. She didn't blame her, really. How could she? Blythe had shown up unannounced and interrupted their obvious plans. She should leave, but she couldn't move as she watched the woman stroll past Finn. "You know I won't be back, right?" she asked with a hateful tone, though the question was filled with hope. She wanted Finn to ask her to stay. To change his mind.

He nodded, looking above her head with a stiff jaw as he responded. "Yep."

The woman offered a feigned laugh. "Whatever." She disappeared down the stairwell, her stomping footsteps echoing throughout the hall for what seemed like way too long.

When silence surrounded them, Blythe looked back up at Finn, in awe of what had just happened. What he'd done for her.

"You didn't have to—"

"I know," he confirmed, opening the door wider. "Come in."

"Finn, I'm so sorry. I didn't mean to interrupt."

"I know that, too," he told her. "And it's okay. What's going on?"

"What do you mean?"

He sat down on the arm of his couch, locking his

fingers together and resting his hands on his knees. "I mean...it's been over a month, Blythe. What are you doing here?"

"I'm sorry," she said. "I don't know why I came here. I didn't know where else to go."

"Problems with your aunt?"

"No," she answered, surprised at just how much he remembered. She wouldn't have been shocked if he didn't even recognize her at all. It was one insignificant night... but he seemed to be just as drawn to her as she was to him. Maybe the night meant more to them both than she'd previously realized.

"Then what?" he asked. "Talk to me."

"It doesn't matter. It's stupid."

He stood, walking toward her slowly. "If it's gotten you this upset, it's not stupid." He placed a careful hand on her arm, caressing her gently. "Are you hurt?"

"No," she answered quickly. "No, it's just...you're going to think I'm ridiculous." She bit her lip. "I guess I probably am ridiculous. I had a...I guess a fight. With a guy."

He dropped his hand from her arm instantly, but the warm expression didn't leave his face. "A boyfriend?"

"No. Er, well, I don't know. I've only known him for two weeks. I thought he wanted to date me seriously, but I guess it wasn't too serious for him. He was seeing someone else. Multiple *someone elses*, probably."

"He was cheating on you?"

"He says it wasn't cheating. I guess he just doesn't want to be exclusive. Which...whatever, ya know? I just...I didn't realize it." She looked back up at him, studying his deep brown eyes and trying to judge his expression. Did he think she was ridiculous? Did he think she was being childish? Did he think she was wasting his time?

His hand was back on her arm, interrupting her thoughts. "He's an idiot."

"W-what?" she asked, his statement catching her off guard and causing a laugh to erupt from her throat.

"Blythe, look, the guy's obviously an idiot. If he had the chance to be with you and he threw that all away for someone else—for *anyone* else—then he's not worthy of any of this."

She rolled her eyes. "You're being sweet. Thank you for saying that."

"I'm being honest."

"Was I stupid? I mean, should I have known that it wasn't exclusive? He never said it was. He never said anything."

"You aren't stupid, Blythe. This isn't your fault."

"I just...I know the cool thing right now, for whatever reason, is to act like I don't care a thing about finding love. People our age are supposed to be tough and independent and think that love is the last thing on our mind because we'd rather run away from it than ever get hurt. It's what every song is about, and all the best movies. I get it. I really, really do. But I don't care about that. Because I do care about love. I'd rather be hurt a thousand times than give up on the idea of finding love and being truly happy. You know? That's not me. I don't care if it makes me seem desperate. What is the point of all of this heartbreak and loneliness? What is the point of even living if we aren't out there looking for an eventual happily ever after?" She let out a heavy breath, exhausted from speaking for so long without air. "I know that's not what guys want to hear—"

"Stop," he told her. "Stop making excuses for how you feel, Blythe. You're allowed to want what you want. Plain and simple. If this guy couldn't give you what you want, someone else will."

She offered him a sad smile. It hadn't gone over her head that his hand was off of her arm once again. Someone else would make her happy. But not Asher. Not Finn. She'd freaked him out. She'd released her full crazy, and he was officially terrified. She could see it in his eyes.

"I'm sorry. I shouldn't be venting this all to you," she said with exhaustion. "I don't even know why I'm here."

He walked past her toward the kitchen area, and she spun around watching him open the fridge and pull out one beer, and then another. "Well, as long as you're here, we may as well have a good time."

She took the beer from his hand after he opened it. "Thank you."

He nodded as he twisted his own top off, taking a drink and sucking the liquid from his upper lip. "No problem. When you were here before, I told you you could come back anytime you needed." He tipped his head toward her. "I meant that."

"I didn't think I'd need to come back."

He took another slow drink. "I hoped you would."

"I didn't mean to interrupt your date."

"It wasn't a date, Blythe. She was just a girl."

"So...not *exclusive*, right?" she asked, suddenly feeling bad for the woman who'd left. It was obvious they were going to sleep together, if they hadn't already. Had she put that poor woman through what Asher had done to her?

"Not exclusive because we weren't dating. We were just...messing around, I guess."

She scowled, though she tried to hide it, and he smirked. "I know that's not what you want to hear."

"What do you mean?"

"You want that happily ever after, and you're trying hard to believe that not all guys are the jerks that this guy was."

She waited for him to deny it, but he didn't. "Is there a 'but' coming?"

He set his beer down on the counter. "Yeah, he'll come around someday, maybe."

She nodded, taking a drink and letting the cool beverage calm her racing heart. "Okay," she said, because what else was there to say?

"Someday you'll meet someone who wants the same things that you do, Blythe. And you may get hurt along the way, but if it's worth the risk to you, then more power to you. You'll find him. Screw this guy."

She sucked in a breath, feeling betrayed by the disappointment she felt. It wasn't like she was hoping Finn would take her in his arms and declare his love for her, but somehow that possibility wouldn't have been the worst thing. He was clearly drawing the line, though. *Someday* she'd meet someone. Not a month ago. That *someone* wasn't him.

"So, what should we do?"

He frowned. "What would you like to do?"

54

"Honestly, I'm exhausted and starving. I'm a pretty lame date, I guess. It's been a long day."

He patted the counter. "Oh, thank God." She lowered her brow, waiting for an explanation. "I worked all morning, and honestly, I'm pretty tired, too. If you said you wanted to go out, I was going to put on my dancing shoes and take you out, but my God, I was going to hate it." He laughed, a hand on his stomach. She couldn't get over how much his laugh warmed her.

"Well, that's incredibly nice of you, but I won't subject either of us to such torture."

"I appreciate it," he told her, leaning over the counter into a bow.

"So...should I go, then?"

"Up to you," he said simply. "I'm in no way ready to entertain, but if you're okay with a low-key night in, you're welcome to stay."

She lit up at his words. "I would love to stay."

"Say no more," he told her, pulling out his cell phone. "What are you craving? Pizza, okay? We'll order in and watch terrible TV and probably crash way too early. I told you I'm pretty lame tonight."

"Are you sure you're okay with that?" she asked.

"Shhh," he silenced her, already on the phone and ordering a pizza. She turned away from him, walking back toward the living room to settle onto the couch with a growing smile on her face.

Once the pizza had been ordered, he sank down beside her, seeming completely at ease. How she longed to feel the same, but she couldn't ignore the electricity pulsing through her body. She tried to think of Asher and how she must only feel this way because Finn was there for her when she needed him—twice now, in fact—but thinking of Asher only made her feel sick, so she let her mind wander.

"So…" Finn said, breaking up the silence. He set his beer on the coffee table and propped his feet up, placing his hands behind his head. "How are you liking New York so far?"

"Much better than my first day," she said. "That's for sure."

"But not better than your second, right?" he joked.

She smirked. "I'm surprised we haven't run into each other, honestly."

"It's a big city," he reminded her. "Unless you want to find someone, you usually don't."

She paused. "You didn't want to find me?" she asked, surprising herself with the question.

He stared at her, his face serious. He seemed to be contemplating what to say next, his gaze darting back and forth between her eyes. He opened his mouth but shut it again. Suddenly, before she realized what was happening, he leaned down, his knuckle under her chin as he lifted her mouth to his. His stubble scraped her skin, his lips warm against hers as she sank into the kiss. She let out a breath through her nose, wrapping her arms around his neck—careful not to spill the beer in her hand.

He cradled her face with both hands, his touch delicate but commanding. When they broke apart, both gasping for air, it was too soon. She stared at him with wide eyes, her forefinger on her lips as she waited for him to make the next move.

"Does that answer your question?" he asked, picking up the beer again and grabbing the remote.

"Mhm," she said, still trying to collect her racing thoughts. He'd answered her question and given her so many more.

CHAPTER EIGHT

The next morning, Blythe woke up next to Finn in his bed. His arm was pinned underneath her and her head rested comfortably on his chest. They hadn't slept together—not that she hadn't wanted to—but she had managed to get one more mind-blowing kiss after the pizza just before they'd both crashed. They were exhausted, after all. It was nice how comfortable they were with each other, she thought. It was nice that despite her anxiety, which had settled some, her mind could find a bit of solace in his arms and quiet enough for her to fall asleep and forget, just for the moment, about the heartbreak she'd experienced a few hours before.

When she sat up, he stirred, rubbing a hand over his face as his eyes focused on her. He seemed confused at first, but a smile quickly found its way to his lips.

"Hey," he whispered, his voice coated in sleep.

"Hey," she said, leaning over onto one arm.

"How'd you sleep?"

"Like a baby," she answered honestly.

"I'm glad," he told her. They didn't touch, and he didn't move in for a kiss, but the look in his eyes told her their intimate—albeit small—moments from the night before hadn't been forgotten. He looked over at his phone, picking it up from the nightstand littered with receipts and water bottles and letting out a yawn. "I have to be at work soon."

"Right," she said, staring around the room for her own phone. Where had she left it?

"What are your plans for the day?"

"I have to work, too," she said. It was true, though she was thinking incredibly hard about calling in sick.

"When will you be off?" he asked, pushing himself up off the bed and throwing on a shirt.

"Late," she said. "Ten-ish, maybe. Depending on how quickly we get everything cleaned up."

He let out another yawn before leaning down and kissing her lips quickly. "Long day."

"Mhm," she mumbled. When he pulled away, she stood from the bed, noticing her phone lying on the floor. She picked it up and slid it into her back pocket. "Well, I guess I'll get going."

He nodded. "Want some coffee before you leave?"

"I'm okay, thanks," she said stiffly, unable to hide the frustration in her voice. She was being dismissed. Clearly last night hadn't meant to him half of what it had meant to her.

"Sure," he said, walking down the hallway. She followed closely behind, flicking through several Facebook notifications and a text message from Asher.

Can we talk?

"The guy?" Finn asked, interrupting her thoughts.

"What?"

"He texted you, right?"

"How do you know?"

"Why wouldn't he?" Finn asked, a sad smile on his face. Or was it her imagination that it was sad?

"Yeah, he wants to talk."

"What are you going to do?"

"I don't know…" she said honestly. She wanted Finn to give her a reason not to talk to Asher again. To tell her that he was going to fight for her. That she deserved better. Instead, he nodded and opened the door. "You think I should talk to him?"

He let out a breath, rubbing the sleep from his eye. She liked the way his hair was a mess in the morning, even messier than hers, surprisingly enough. "I think the guy is a jerk, Blythe, but he's not my boyfriend."

"He's not my boyfriend either," she said. *Apparently.* "Look, Finn…about last night…" She trailed off, hoping he would finish her sentence.

"It doesn't have to mean anything," he told her. "You were confused and upset."

"I was," she said. "But not about that. Not about what happened between us."

"We kissed, Blythe. You can say the word."

"We did kiss," she confirmed.

"Like I said, it doesn't have to mean anything."

"Did it, though?" she asked. "To you?"

He rolled his head back, covering his eyes. "It's too early in the morning for this conversation," he said, adding a yawn for emphasis.

"Okay," she said finally, her pride taking a hit as she walked past him. "Thanks for letting me stay here last night, Finn. I'll see you. Maybe." She lowered her head as she walked away.

"Blythe, wait," he called, his voice sending a wave of hope through her. She spun around.

"Yeah?"

"If he's still *not* your boyfriend when you get off work, come back."

Her jaw nearly dropped as she said the words. "Come back here?"

"What else would I mean by that?"

A smile grew on her face. "Okay," she practically screamed, her voice way too perky. "I will."

He scowled, looking a bit happy in spite of himself. "Don't read too much into it…or whatever."

She nodded, unable to tame her smile. "See you tonight."

"Yeah, yeah," he muttered, turning away and shutting the door. She hadn't missed the brilliant smile that had grown on his face as he dismissed her.

CHAPTER NINE

At work that night, Blythe moved with a lightness she hadn't known in a while—maybe her whole life. That was what falling in love was like, wasn't it? Light. Shining through you. Lifting you up. No matter how many times you fall in love, every single time always feels like it's the first. Like this time is somehow different. Somehow better. Okay, so she wasn't falling in love just yet, but that didn't stop the expanding feeling her heart had claimed for its own. She watched the clock, the hands moving slower and slower as she grew closer to the end of the party.

At just past eight, one of her female coworkers, Tyler, approached her. "Hey, Blythe, there's someone outside for you."

"What?" she asked. No one in New York knew her. Except her aunt, and why wouldn't she call? Well, her aunt or Finn. Or Asher. She hated the hope that fluttered through her at the thought of Asher. She'd chosen not to respond to his text and she'd ignored the phone call that came through around noon, but he'd made no further attempts to contact her. It wasn't him. Probably. "Can you cover?" she asked, turning to head back toward the kitchen.

"Sure," Tyler responded. "Go ahead."

She walked through the swinging door that led into the kitchen and set her empty tray down. As she walked toward the back of the house, she spied him through the glass of the storm door. "Asher?"

He nodded, his eyes narrowing as he saw her, an uncertain smile spreading across his cheeks. "Hi," he said.

"What are you doing here?"

"I tried to call."

"Yeah, I saw."

"You're ignoring me?" he asked.

She twisted her mouth in thought. "I'm not ignoring you, I just need time to figure out what I want."

"I know. I assumed." He stuck his hands in his pockets. "Look, can we just…talk?" he asked, reaching for the door handle. She nodded, stepping out as he pulled it open.

"What do you want to talk about?"

He sighed. "About how much of an idiot I am." His words surprised her. His face showed a small, hopeful smile as he waited for her to speak. When she didn't, he went on. "I'm sorry if I hurt you. I'm sorry if what happened took you by surp—"

"You don't have to do this," she interrupted.

"No, I want to." He took a breath, reaching for her hand. "When you walked away from me last night, I realized something I hadn't until that point. I'm crazy about you, Blythe, and that scares me. We haven't known each other long, not long enough for me to feel this way about you. But I do. And what scares me even more is the idea of you walking away for good and me never seeing you again. I…I don't know if I could do that."

She furrowed her brow. "So, what are you saying?"

"I'm saying…if you need us to be exclusive, I think I can do that."

"I don't want to give you an ultimatum, Asher. That's not the point. Last night just surprised me. I assumed we were exclusive, and that was my fault—"

"No, no it wasn't. I should've been more clear."

She patted the top of his hand with hers. "It was both of our faults. But, to be honest, I'm not sure that I can do the non-exclusive thing. That still may be a dealbreaker for me."

"Then I'll—"

"But," she held up a hand, "even more than that, I can't feel like I've forced you."

"So, what are you saying?" he asked, scratching the back of his neck.

"I…I just need time, Asher. I need space to figure everything out. I do like you. I do want to see you again, but I need—"

He grabbed her hands, kissing her fingers softly. "So, will you see me tomorrow?"

"I work," she told him, picking at a piece of skin around her fingernail.

"Oh," he said sadly. "Okay."

"But, I'm off the next day," she offered. "I could meet you for lunch."

"Lunch would be great," he said, his expression filled

with joy. He looked like a puppy dog that had been handed a bone, and she couldn't help being flattered by his persistence.

"Okay."

He leaned forward, his lips brushing hers with a light kiss. "I'm going to make this up to you, Blythe."

She smiled, letting go of his hand and grabbing the door handle with blushing cheeks. "Just text me the details."

CHAPTER TEN

After work that night, feeling more exhilarating than exhausted, Blythe made her way across town in a hurry. Though she still had Asher's words flowing through her mind, the promise of returning to Finn's place hadn't left her thoughts since she'd walked out of his building that morning. She couldn't understand why she was so excited to see him, but she was. There was no denying the effect he had on her; though Asher had a similar one. She'd thought she'd given up one option to be able to take another, but Asher had changed his mind. Where exactly did that leave her?

She couldn't stand the idea of choosing either one of them—if Finn was even an option in the first place. He hadn't said for sure. In fact, he'd told her specifically not to read too much into it. But that kiss hadn't been nothing. His touch had sent lightning to her toes...surely he'd felt it, too? She needed to see where Finn stood before she could make a decision. She needed to know if he was even putting himself in the running.

As she approached his building, taking the steps two at a time, she landed on his floor with excitement ready to explode in her chest. She knocked twice, surprised when he answered almost immediately.

He'd showered, his hair still slightly wet and the apartment smelling of soap. He was dressed in a black T-shirt and jeans, not too dressed up but not entirely casual. "Hey," he said, his voice raised slightly. He'd been waiting for her. Pacing by the door, maybe, if his speed in answering it were any indication. She stepped inside the apartment.

"Hi," she told him, staring at him awkwardly. Should she go in for a hug? Another kiss? It felt strange to do nothing. Luckily, he eased her worries by shutting the door and running a hand through his hair.

"How was…um, how was work?"

"Work was okay," she said, setting down her purse.

"I wasn't sure if you wanted to stay in or go out."

She looked at her clothes, a white blouse with black vest and black pants. "We can go out," she said, "but let me just change out of my work clothes."

"Sure," he told her, stepping out of her way so that she could disappear down the hallway. He noticed something still slung over one shoulder he hadn't seen when she arrived.

She pulled the simple black sundress from her bag, sliding it over her shoulders and pulling her hair down from her bun. Her wavy hair fell down her back, still imprinted from the updo she'd sported all day. She reached in her bag and pulled out a hairbrush, running it through her locks in an attempt to tame them. When she'd managed to force them into looking somewhat decent, she put on an extra coat of Chapstick, deodorant, and mascara. She wasn't date-ready by any means, but it would do.

"Do you even have clothes?" he asked, shocking her as his voice came from the opposite side of the closed door.

"I stopped before work to pick up some things," she told him. "I wasn't sure if I'd be staying, but I packed for it just in case."

He was silent for a moment, and she worried if she'd assumed wrong. "You can stay for as long as you need to, Blythe," he said eventually. "I've told you that before."

She opened the bedroom door, staring at him. "Thank you."

He nodded, stepping back as his eyes trailed down her body to where the hem of her dress met her tanned legs. "Did, uh," he looked back up to meet her eyes, "I'm assuming you never heard from the guy?"

She cleared her throat. "I did, actually."

"You did?" he asked. His tone wasn't shocked or angry, which left her unsure how to feel. "How did it go?"

"He wants to get back together. Exclusively." Her eyes darted between his, trying to judge his guarded expression.

"So…are you going to?"

She shrugged. "I told him I needed time."

"I see."

"Because I wanted to see…I mean, I don't want to assume…" She held out a hand, hoping she wouldn't have to elaborate and make a fool of herself if she was wrong. When it became obvious he wasn't going to help her out, she sucked in a deep breath. "I didn't know what to tell him about us."

He eased down the hallway, looking back over his shoulder as he spoke. "I don't think there's anything to tell."

"There's not?" she asked.

He turned back around to face her, his eyes on her lips. "Do you want there to be?"

"I mean, last night wasn't nothing to me. It meant something." He nodded but didn't respond. "Did it mean something to you?" she asked.

He looked down, then back up, meeting her eyes. "Of course it did," he said. "But I don't want to promise you something I can't give."

"What do you mean?" she asked.

"I...look, I do like you, Blythe. But I'm not in a place for a relationship."

"Oh," she said, taking a step back from him as cool tears stung her eyes. She was embarrassed. What had she been thinking? "Okay."

"Don't be upset," he told her, reaching for her arm.

"What was this, then, Finn? What was tonight? Why would you invite me back? You just thought you could sleep with me and send me away like the girl from last night?"

He let out a soft laugh, then his face went serious again. "I wasn't going to sleep with you, Blythe."

"Why is that funny?" she demanded.

"It's not funny. You're right that I shouldn't have invited you here without explaining why I was. You were confused about everything with your boyfriend, and I didn't want to add to that. But…I wanted to see you again."

"I wanted to see you, too."

"But I can't date you."

"Why?" she asked.

"Because…you made it clear last night that you are looking for something serious."

She nodded with her lips pressed firmly together, slapping her leg. "Great. So, I scared you off."

"It's not that," he said. "It's just…it wouldn't be fair to you to let you come into this expecting more than I can offer. I know what I bring to the table, and stability doesn't come with my territory. I do like you, but, more than that, I care about you, so I want to be fair to your feelings."

"I don't understand."

"I know," he told her. "And I don't expect you to."

"So, that's it? You're just taking yourself out of the running?"

"I don't deserve to be in the running with a girl like you."

She sank onto the arm of the couch. "A girl like me?" she demanded. "What's *that* supposed to mean?"

"You're just…I don't know. You're special."

"Thanks, *Dad*," she teased, feeling sad at the thought of her own dad.

"You know what I mean."

"No. I don't," she insisted. "Because what you're saying is ridiculous. What? I'm too good for you? You have your own apartment. You have a job. You took care of me when I was just a stranger. You've offered to let me stay here despite the fact that I'm still *basically* a stranger. What part of you is bad?"

"I didn't say I was bad," he said quickly. "I'm not a bad guy."

"I know that."

"It's just…I'm not stable. I'm not the best choice for you. But that doesn't mean I don't wish I was. I want to be selfish, but you deserve more than that."

"I decide what I deserve, Finn," she told him, poking his chest with her finger. "No one else."

"Look, all I'm saying is that if you want happily ever after, you should choose someone else. I'm not that guy."

She nodded, her throat tight. "Fair enough."

"So, do you still want to go out, or…"

"Do *you* still want to?"

He smirked. "I'm starving."

"Okay, then." She stood, watching as his expression filled with relief and he turned around, pulling open the door. When she drew close to him, he reached for her arm, stopping her before she passed through the door. She looked to her right, staring into his dark eyes as a fire lit in her belly. His lips parted slightly, his eyes darting between hers.

"Blythe, I—"

"Yeah?" she asked when he didn't finish his sentence right away.

"I do want to be an option," he said firmly. "I may be the wrong one. But I'll hate myself if I don't at least say that I want to be in the running."

She leaned forward, pressing her lips to his without warning. "Keep it up, and you may just be in the lead."

CHAPTER ELEVEN

The next day, Blythe laid on the couch wearing Finn's sweatpants and T-shirt. At the end of their date, he'd offered them to her, and though she had her own, she felt extra safe wearing his. There'd been a few more kisses, though nothing serious despite their amazing night. He was holding her at arm's length, and she couldn't for the life of her understand why.

A knock on the door startled her, and she sat up straight, looking around the empty apartment. Finn had just run out to get them breakfast from a cafe across the street, but she wasn't sure why he'd be knocking. The knock came again, this time louder, and she stood, walking toward the door slowly.

"Finn—open the damn door!" called a gruff voice. She jumped back, bumping into the stool behind his kitchen island and knocking it over. "Damn it! I can hear you in there!" the voice called again, pounding on the door for a third time.

"Sorry!" she called, approaching the door and staring

out through the peephole. "I'm sorry. Finn isn't here right now."

"Like hell he isn't."

"No, he's really not." She stared at the man through the blurred glass, taking in his bulky form, his long white beard, and the leather vest on his muscled shoulders. He snarled his lips at her, though she knew he couldn't see her.

"Where is he, then?" he asked.

"He went to get breakfast. He'll be back. I can tell him you stopped by."

"No. I'll wait," he said angrily. "Are you going to let me in or what?" His fist collided with the wood of the door, shaking it in the frame.

"Who are you?" she asked.

"I'm—"

"What the hell are you doing here?" Finn's voice shocked them both as it climbed the stairwell. She tried hard to find him in the small line of vision the peephole allowed her.

"I should ask you the same thing. You weren't even going to contact me? I had to find out you lived here from Jack."

"Yeah, with good reason," Finn said angrily. "What are you doing here?"

"What kind of a hello is that after all these years?"

"It's not," Finn spat. "You aren't welcome here."

The man folded his arms across his chest, and Blythe spied a sleeve of tattoos on his bicep. "You don't even know all that's happened since you've been gone."

"I don't have to know, Tommy. Jack should've never told you where I live. He knew that."

"Well, he did. So whatcha gonna do about it? Move?"

"I'm not running," he said firmly. Finn squared shoulders with the man, no fear evident in his eyes though he was less than half the size of the boulder of a man. They stood roughly the same height, but Tommy looked like he spent his life in a gym, while Finn was leaner.

Tommy scoffed, shaking his head. "You always were a stupid little shit, weren't you?"

"Do you need something? I don't have any money."

"Figures," he said, blowing a breath of air out his nose. "I can see you're...busy...anyway." He gestured toward the door. "What do you say I come back?"

"The answer will be the same then. Get out of my doorway and leave me alone."

"We'll see about that," he said, but to Blythe's surprise he stepped aside, letting Finn pass.

Finn put his key in the lock, looking over his shoulder to make sure the man was walking away before opening the door. When he entered the apartment, it was with a sudden burst of adrenaline, and he slammed it shut just as quickly, locking the two deadbolts. When he looked at her, his eyes were wild with fear. "Did he hurt you? Did he say anything to you?"

"No, I'm fine. Who was that?"

Finn leaned his back against the door, sliding down slightly and letting out a breath as he stared at the ceiling. The man had rattled him much more than he'd let on in the hallway. After a moment, he pushed off from the door, moving to the counter to empty the brown paper sack in his hand.

"Everything bagel and sweet tea, just like you requested." He set the food down, walking down the hall away from her without offering an answer.

"Finn?" she called after him, not bothering to touch her food. "Are you okay?"

When he reached the door, he glanced at her, offering a small smile. "I'm fine," he assured her. "Just give me a sec, okay?"

She nodded. "O-okay," she replied, but the door was already creaking shut with him on the other side. She returned to her bagel, her stomach growling despite the fact that her mind was on anything but food at that moment.

She picked at her food, taking a sip of the tea that made her miss home so much. It had been so long since she'd even thought about home. New York consumed her mind. There was so much to do and see, think about and talk about, and Texas had taken a backseat to her new home. But the tea made her miss it, despite the fact that it wasn't true sweet tea. Not the kind she was used to. The sugar had been added in once it had cooled, she could tell. A typical mistake in the North, but one her Southern tongue recognized immediately.

The door to the bedroom opened and Finn emerged, back in his pajamas. He walked past the food he'd gotten for himself and sank onto the couch, a haunted expression on his face.

She walked toward him, sitting on the cushion next to

him and placing her hand on his knee. "Should I be worried?"

He looked up at her, and she expected him to cast her fears aside, but instead he frowned. "I'm sorry, Blythe."

"What are you sorry fo—"

"I'm so sorry. I never should've left you here alone."

"I was fine."

"You might not have been. I'd never forgive myself if something had happened to you."

She took his face in her hands, forcing him to look at her. "Nothing happened, Finn. I'm fine. I knew better than to open the door."

"He'd've gotten in if he wanted to." He sighed, running his palm over his face as he pulled away from her hands.

"But he didn't. Are you going to tell me who he is, anyway?"

"Someone from my past," he said simply. "Someone I never wanted to see again."

"How did he find you?" she asked. "Who is 'Jack'? The man who told him where you live."

He furrowed his brow. "Jack is...someone I used to know. Look, I'll handle it, okay? I don't want you involved."

"Involved in what? Are you...is something dangerous going on?"

He looked down, taking her hand in his with a grimace on his face. "I want you to leave, Blythe."

"W-what?" she asked with a half laugh. She was sure he was kidding because it was so out of the blue. "What are you talking about?"

"You need to leave. I can't see you anymore."

"No," she said softly, her heart fluttering at the mere possibility. "Why?"

"Because I've put you in danger, and I can't have that."

"I'm not afraid," she tried to argue.

"It doesn't matter," he said sternly, his voice raised in frustration. "It doesn't matter how you feel. How either of us feel. You need to leave. Now. I'm revoking my offer for you to stay. You have to leave, and you can never come back here. Do you hear me?" He stood from the couch, walking across the room.

"Because you don't want me here, or because I'm in danger?"

"You aren't in danger. They have no idea who you are, and I'm going to make sure it stays that way."

"Who are *they*? I don't want to leave, Finn…"

"Damn it, Blythe," he said, slamming his fist onto the back of the couch. He lowered his voice when he saw the fear that filled her eyes. Her father had been soft spoken, even in the most trying times. A man's voice being raised caused her to hyperventilate, and it usually ended in tears. "I'm sorry, okay? I'm so sorry."

"Don't be sorry," she whispered. "Just…tell me what's going on."

He walked toward the bedroom, and she wondered if he might be going to get some vital piece of the puzzle that would explain this alternate universe she seemed to have stepped into, but when he returned, he was carrying her bag. "You need to leave."

She nodded, setting her drink on the coffee table and taking the bag from his hands without another word. She knew when she wasn't welcome. She walked toward the door and pulled it open.

"Blythe, I—" She turned, studying his conflicted expression. He looked down. "Goodbye."

She stepped through the door. "Goodbye, Finn."

CHAPTER TWELVE

"You came," Asher said, standing up from the table as she entered the restaurant.

"Are you surprised?"

"I am, actually," he said with a laugh, placing an arm around her waist as he kissed her cheek.

"I wouldn't have made the plans if I wasn't going to follow through, Asher." She sank into the chair. "How are you?"

"I'm…better now," he told her, taking a seat after she did. "Have you had a chance to think about what I said?"

She nodded. "I miss seeing you."

He let out a sigh of relief, reaching across the table to take her hand. "I miss seeing you, too."

"But I'm still not sure I want to be exclusive. I don't want to feel like I'm forcing you."

He kissed her fingertips. "You aren't, though, Blythe. You aren't."

She took a sip of the wine that was waiting in her glass, impressed that he remembered her preference of red over white. *With so many girls to keep track of, anyway.* She dismissed the thought from her mind. "So, in your text you said you had something you wanted to talk to me about?"

He took a drink, as if trying to gain a bit of liquid courage, and rubbed his hands together, adjusting in his seat. "I do." He paused. "I know we are still in a weird place, and I know you don't trust me yet, but I really like you, Blythe. Like, really, really like you. I didn't realize it until you walked away from me. I haven't been able to stop thinking about you. I'm not dating anyone else. I'm all-in with you."

It seemed fast for someone who hadn't wanted anything serious just a few days before. Blythe stared at him. "Are you saying that because you think it's what I want to hear?"

"I'm saying it because it's true. Now, it doesn't mean I'm ready for major commitment. I'm still young, and I don't plan to settle down for a few years."

"I'm not looking for a marriage, Asher. That's not what—"

"I know," he interrupted, holding up a hand. "Just...let me finish. I've never really been in a serious relationship. I like to keep my options open. I always have. My parents didn't always have a great relationship—it's not an excuse, I'm just trying to explain—so, when you said you wanted to be exclusive, I panicked. No girl has ever expected that from me. But, then you walked away and the thought of being without you...even with the possibility of being with thirty other women...it was terrifying. I don't want to be with anyone else if it means I can't be with you." He ran a thumb over her knuckles, taking a deep breath. She was losing herself in his eyes, the candlelight on their tabletop dancing in the black irises. "So, to prove to you just how serious I am…I wanted to ask if you'd consider going to a cabin with me Upstate this weekend. I know it's last minute, but if you can get off work, I promise to make it worth your while."

She was completely thrown off by the proposition, expecting literally anything else to have come from his mouth. "W-what?"

"My parents are hosting a party for my grandmother's eightieth birthday. I've never brought a girl home to meet my family. But…I want you to come."

She smiled, the idea filling her belly with a weird mix of excitement and nerves. "I don't know…"

"Come on," he coaxed. "You'll love it. We own a few vacation cabins all there together. It's really beautiful. And if you hate it, you don't have to stay. I'll bring you home or call you a car. But you won't hate it."

She thought for a moment, trying to picture herself 'Upstate,' as he called it. It seemed like something she'd hear in a movie. A cabin in the mountains? It may as well have been a screensaver.

"You're smiling…" he whispered, brushing her cheek with his outstretched fingertips. "Is that a good sign?" He was right, she realized, as her hand went to her lips. She nodded slowly.

"Okay."

"Yeah?"

"Mhm," she confirmed. "I'll go."

He leaned across the table, bumping into it noisily as

his mouth searched for hers. She pressed her lips into his kiss, welcoming it as her heart thudded in her chest.

"What are you doing to me, woman?" Asher asked as they pulled away, his awestruck gaze locked on her.

She smirked, taking a sip of her wine as the waiter approached their table. "Teaching you to bend."

THE CAR RIDE north was filled with laughter. Despite her worries about Finn, she was trying hard to focus on the man who *did* seem to want her. Luckily, he hadn't made it too difficult. On top of keeping her entertained, Asher had packed enough food to feed a kindergarten class on a week-long fieldtrip. And he'd shopped like one, too. Bags of Twizzlers, M&Ms, Skittles, Bugles, Doritos, and Reese's Minis lined the floor of the rented BMW.

Blythe sat with her legs crossed in the seat, chewing on an orange Twizzler.

"I can't believe you like those," he said with a laugh. "I thought you were joking when you asked for 'em."

She wiggled the candy in the air. "They're my favorite. Orange cream anything...mmmmm." She snorted as she took another bite.

"Your favorite snack? Or your favorite food in general?" he asked.

"My favorite snack," she told him, and when he feigned a sigh of relief, she went on, "my second favorite food."

"Do I want to know your first?"

"French fries, of course!" she said, appearing appalled.

He laughed. "Of course. I forgot I was dating a toddler."

"What about you? What's your favorite food? Caviar?"

He rolled his eyes at her, snatching the bag of Twizzlers and threatening to throw them out the window 'if she was going to be so sassy.' She laughed loudly, begging for the bag back. "I'm sorry, I'm sorry!"

He tossed the bag back to her. "For your information, my favorite food is pizza."

"Really?"

Asher nodded. "Don't look so surprised. New York has some of the best pizza in the world."

"I just assumed you'd have expensive taste."

"And I just assumed your favorite food would be fried chicken and *mashed taters*," he teased, assuming a fake Southern drawl.

"Fair enough," she relented. "What about your second favorite?"

"Now, *that's* caviar." She stared at him for a moment, realizing he was joking and laughing again until her stomach burned and her eyes watered. When she'd calmed, he cleared his throat. "No, but seriously, when I was a kid I *only* ate pizza. Like, it was the only food group in my life."

"That sounds…super unhealthy."

"It totally was. My parents had this world-class chef, and literally the only thing he could fix that I would eat was pizza. I even got creative when my parents told me I couldn't request pizza anymore and started asking him to make 'azzip.'"

She furrowed her brow, taking another bite of her Twizzler. "Azzip? What's that?"

"Azzip. Backwards pizza," he said with a laugh. He held his hand out flat in front of his mouth as if he were eating a slice of pizza and rotated his hand so that his fingers were closest to his lips before giving her a wink. "I invented it when I was seven."

"Oh my God, that's either completely terrible or complete genius."

He patted his chest. "Well, my parents didn't find it nearly as funny. Needless to say, my belt is very grateful that they pretty much banned pizza from our house after that. But if I'm given the choice, pizza is still my number one." He pointed to the sky, pretending to have tears in his eyes.

She rolled her eyes. "You're funny, Asher Grace. Why didn't I realize you were funny before?"

He lowered the volume of a John Legend song on the radio as they slowed to turn onto a new street. "I guess I was trying too hard to impress you before."

"You didn't think this would impress me?"

He shook his head. "Nah, girls don't want funny guys. I mean, sure, every girl says they do, but only when that funny guy also has six-pack abs, a chiseled jaw, and a few extra zeros in his bank account."

She dropped her jaw. "But you have all of those things, Asher."

"I know," he said sheepishly. "But a guy can only show off so many things at once. And speaking of showing off..." He pointed out the window, and her gaze followed his finger, looking out as a line of three houses came into view.

House was a bit of an understatement, if she was being honest. *Cabin* didn't even come close. What she was staring at were nothing short of rustic mansions with scenic views of snow-capped mountains. Large, picturesque windows lined the front of each house, giving a darkened view of whatever was happening inside. Dark-cherry stained wood sided each building, leading out to balconies that overlooked the thick forests behind the houses. It looked like something from a magazine. Something from a dream.

"Whoa," Blythe said, plopping her feet onto the floorboard as she leaned forward to get a better view. "This is incredible."

"Yeah," Asher agreed, pulling down a long, gravel driveway.

"Forget funny. You should've led with this."

CHAPTER THIRTEEN

Asher led Blythe into the middle house, insisting on carrying her bag inside. When they walked through the door, Blythe let out another gasp. It was beautiful—not that she was surprised. Rustic, yet modern, the perfect mix of wood-lined walls, fur rugs, and gold-plated art. The glass windows gave her a gorgeous view of the land surrounding the house, and it was enough for her to spend a full day taking it all in.

"Beautiful, isn't it?" Asher asked, setting their bags down and walking up behind her, one hand on her waist. He spun her around, pressing her back to the glass and lowering his lips to hers slowly. The kiss was sensual in a way he hadn't been before. He was in his element here. Or maybe it was just her change of heart. Either way, it had a chill running down to her toes.

His palms trailed around the hem of her shirt, his thumbs sliding under the fabric to meet her skin. Her tongue danced with his as he let out a low moan and leaned in further. Their legs were tangled, breaths growing faster when she pushed him away gently.

"Asher," she scolded, pulling her shirt down. "We can't do this here."

"Why not?" he asked, twirling a piece of her hair around his finger.

"What if your parents see? That is *not* how I plan to meet them."

"No one's here yet," he told her. "My parents won't be here until this evening, and the caterers and event planners still have an hour before they show up."

"Event planners? For a birthday party?"

"Mhm," he said, biting his lip as his hand slid up her shirt again. "Now, do you want to keep talking or should we finish what we—"

"Please don't finish anything," a man's voice said from behind Asher. He whipped his hand out of her shirt, turning around in a flash.

"Dad?" he asked.

"Don't mind me," the man said, a friendly smile on his face. He stood a few inches shorter than Asher, though his posture made him seem taller. He had a full head of salt-and-pepper hair that perfectly matched his well-kept beard. Dressed in khakis and a suit jacket, he was the model of business casual as he reached out his hand to shake his son's, pulling him into a tight hug. "Hello, Son."

"Dad, hi," he said against his shoulder. When they pulled apart, he reached for Blythe's arm, pulling her so that she was standing even with him. "This is Blythe."

"Blythe," his father said, kissing the top of her hand. "You'll forgive me for interrupting."

Her face burned red at his words, but he seemed to be genuine enough. "It's nice to meet you, sir."

"None of this 'sir,' nonsense. You can call me Jacob."

"Right, sorry," Asher said. "This is my father, Jacob." She nodded, placing her hand in her pocket and waiting for Asher to say something else. "We weren't expecting you and Mom until later."

"Yes, I heard," he said, smiling deviously. "But your mother insisted we arrive early. She's hired new caterers, and she wanted to make sure everything ran smoothly."

"How's Grandmother Lorene?"

"She's as sharp as ever," he said, but added, "unfortunately," as he laughed. "Anyway, your mother saw your car pull up, and I'm recruiting you to be my buffer. Sorry, everything else will have to wait. Besides, she's dying to meet the first girl you've ever brought home." He winked playfully at Blythe, and she couldn't help but notice how much he reminded her of Asher.

"Okay, let us get our bags put away," Asher said.

"Fine," Jacob agreed. "Ten minutes and I'll be back." He sighed. "Actually, make it five."

Asher grabbed hold of the bags and began to head up the large staircase on the far side of the room. "You coming?" he asked.

"I'll just...um, I'll wait here," she said awkwardly as Jacob walked out the front door, casting one last sly glance at her.

A few moments later, Asher appeared at the top of the staircase. "I'm so sorry about that."

"It's okay," she said, brushing a piece of hair from her face. "But I'm sure they probably think I'm ruining their son now. Not exactly a picture-perfect way to meet, huh?"

He shook his head, his hand running down the railing of the staircase as he made his way toward her. "Trust me, I was already ruined, and what he just saw doesn't even put a dent in the car wreck that was my teenage years. They've seen me through a lot worse. You're probably the best thing that's ever happened to me. At least, in their eyes," he added at the end, his voice a little higher as if he was worried about what he'd said.

"Well, thanks," she told him, locking her fingers with his as he held his hand out.

"Do you think he'll tell your mom?"

"Nah," he said. "Dad and I...we're cool. He's not gonna rat us out."

"I feel like we're in high school," she said. "Sneaking around and worrying about being caught."

He pulled open the door. "*You* snuck around in high school?"

"As much as the next person," she told him, elbowing him in the side when his eyes bugged out. "Oh come on, what's that supposed to mean?"

"Nothing," he joked, pointing toward the far cabin and leading her that way. "I just picture you as a little goody two-shoes in school."

"I got in my fair share of trouble," she said. "I wasn't a bad kid, though. But I had my rebellious teen years just like everyone else."

He nodded. "Well, if you're lucky, maybe we can spike the punch tonight." The front door opened and Jacob stood in front of them, obviously waiting anxiously. He let out a sigh of quiet relief, turning around with his hands in the air.

"They're here, Mona."

A short woman with bright red lipstick, shoulder-length blonde hair, and a blue mid-length dress rounded a corner, a bright smile plastered on her face.

"She's real!" she exclaimed, hurrying toward Blythe with her arms outstretched. "Come here, come here." A cloud of perfume overtook Blythe's lungs as she was pulled into a tight hug, Mona bobbing her side-to-side with excitement. "Oh my goodness, I can't believe it. When Asher told me he was bringing a girl home with him for the weekend, I thought for sure he was lying. You're real? He didn't, like, hire you or anything?"

"I—I'm real," she said, once her lungs were able to re-inflate to their full size. "It's really nice to meet you, Mrs. Grace."

"Oh, pish-posh, Mrs. Grace. You can call me Mom. Or Mona. But I prefer Mom."

"*Mom*," Asher chided. "Please don't scare her off."

"Scare her off, what about scaring *you* off? What on earth did I ever do to deserve a son who never writes or calls?" She pulled him into another of her spine-crushing hugs, kissing his cheek so that a bright lip print was left.

He wiped it away with the back of his hand. "I'm sorry. Work's just been crazy, you know? It's no excuse."

"Well, you're right about that. But, I'll let it go this time because you've brought a girl home." She pulled Blythe's arm, wrapping hers through the bend and leading her into the kitchen. "Come now, you have to tell me everything. How did you meet? How long have you been together? Do you live together? What do you do? Has he been a gentleman?"

Blythe cast a look over her shoulder to Asher who offered an apologetic shrug. "Take it easy, Mom."

Mona was making no attempt to listen as more and more questions poured from her. Who knew such a small person could contain so much curiosity?

THE PARTY WENT off without a hitch. Continuing to crush every stereotype Blythe had about ridiculously wealthy families, the Graces were the warmest and most welcoming group of people Blythe had ever had the pleasure of meeting. Having grown up in Texas, that was saying a lot. Sure, Mona Grace talked *way* too much, Jacob seemed to always have an all-knowing look in his eye, and Grandmother Lorene asked the same questions over and over again, but they also showered Blythe with attention. In truth, they appeared so relieved to see someone with their son, nothing else seemed to matter.

They'd gracefully overlooked the fact that Blythe felt so out of place surrounded by people who could easily drop on lunch what she'd make in a year. Asher kept her close to him despite mingling with old college buddies, friends of the family, and actual family. Everyone was enthralled to meet her. They wanted to know what she did for a living, what it was like growing up in the South, and how in the world she had ever come to meet 'a man like Asher.' At first, she'd felt self-conscious, as if they believed she wasn't worthy of him and might be questioning how she'd tricked him into spending any time with her, but by the end of the night, she no longer felt as much of an outsider. She'd been introduced to practically everyone there and, for the most part, they'd all been warm and friendly.

As the party wound down and the last few guests began to head out, Grandmother Lorene crept toward her. The woman was in amazing shape for having just turned eighty, and she still seemed to take complete care of herself.

"Well, what'd you think?" she asked.

"What do you mean?" Blythe lowered her brow, trying to hear the woman's voice over the ballad playing through the speakers to her right.

"About the party. What did you think of it?"

"Oh, it was really nice, Grandmother Lorene." It felt like such a formal name, but it was how everyone seemed to address her, Asher and his parents included, so Blythe went with it.

"You could get used to it, eh?" she asked, elbowing her playfully as her eyebrows danced.

"Me?"

"This could be your life now, Blythe. If you nail down our Asher."

"Oh," Blythe said, perhaps a bit too loudly. She put a hand up shaking her head. "It's still...it's still super early, Grandmother Lorene. I don't think we're anywhere close to thinking about that."

The old woman looked across the room to where her grandson stood, his hand on his father's shoulder as he laughed along with a group of middle-aged men. He looked at Blythe, catching her eye for just a moment and smiling warmly. "That boy has never so much as brought a girl home for a Sunday brunch, let alone a party like this."

"Really?" Blythe asked, though she'd already been told the same thing from nearly everyone at the party, including Grandmother Lorene twice now.

"You make him happy. I can see it. I know." She took Blythe's hand, squeezing it in her own. Blythe stared at the translucent skin, purple veins peeking out. "Today's my eightieth birthday party."

"I know," Blythe patronized her. "Happy birthday."

She smiled sadly. "It seems like just last year I was seventeen and falling in love with my husband, Asher's grandfather. Then I was twenty-three with two babies on my hips. Then, I blinked and this could be my last birthday."

"Oh, I'm sure it's not—"

"That's the way life goes," Grandmother Lorene went on, misty tears in her gray eyes. "You make all these plans and think you have all this time. One minute you're planning and the next thing you know you're looking back over it all—at the things you never did, and the things you'd do anything to do again—wondering why you wasted any time making plans when you could've been living. You think you have time, Blythe, but next week you'll be my age." She smiled sadly. "Just...live the best you can, as much as you can, with every second you're given." She pulled her in and kissed her cheek. "This could be your life, sweetheart. And what a life it is."

When she pulled away, she squeezed Blythe's hand one

last time before turning around and darting after a tray of spinach puffs. Blythe met Asher's eyes through the crowd, his face showing concern. She offered up a small smile, trying to hide the tears that had filled her own eyes. *One minute you're planning and the next thing you know you're looking back over it all, wondering why you wasted any time making plans when you could've been living.*

With Grandmother Lorene's words echoing in her head, she thought of her own parents, dead in their mid-forties. They'd made plans. When Blythe graduated, they were going to go on a cruise. Her mother was planning to get her hair cut short for the summer. Her father wanted to buy that new tractor he'd been saving up for. They'd made plans—big and small—and in the end, life didn't seem to care too much about what they hadn't had time to do.

CHAPTER FOURTEEN

When the party was over, the family had a glass of wine together on the balcony, with Mona toasting to the newest 'member of the family' as her eyes twinkled toward Blythe. Once the glasses were empty, Asher began yawning and informed them that they'd had a long drive and they were going to retire 'early.'

In what world one a.m. was considered early, Blythe wasn't sure, but she went with it, saying goodbye to the family and heading out the door with her arm through Asher's.

They walked in silence until they reached their cabin door. Before he opened it, he stopped, staring at her in the moonlight. Shadows covered half of his face and crickets chirped all around them, reminding her of home. It was eerily quiet there, the air thicker somehow.

"I hope tonight wasn't too much," he said softly, interrupting her thoughts. "I know my family can be...overbearing, but they mean well."

"No. Asher, it wasn't too much. Your family...well, they're pretty great."

"That's a stretch," he teased, pushing open the door and letting her in first. "But they really seemed to like you."

"They did?" she asked, though she already assumed. Unless they were tremendous actors.

"Yeah," he said. "I was instructed to make sure you come to the next family function."

"Do you guys do stuff like this a lot?"

He slipped off his jacket and laid it on the back of a rocking chair. "Once or twice a year, maybe. I haven't made it home in the past few years, though."

"Why?" she asked, sitting down in the chair. He sat on the edge of the coffee table, leaning over so that his knees were in front of hers.

"It's just...I was stupid growing up. I made a lot of dumb decisions, and there's a lot of...baggage in our relationship."

"They love you, Asher. Even I could see that."

"No, they do. It's just...you know. Rebellious teenage stuff that I'd rather not deal with now that I'm mature." He dusted his shoulder playfully.

"So, it's awkward?"

He nodded, his lips in a firm line.

"What's the worst thing you've ever done?" she asked, her voice low.

He scowled. "What's the worst thing *you've* ever done?"

"I asked you first."

"You don't want to know that side of me, Blythe."

"I do," she told him, placing a hand on his knee. "I want to know you. All of you."

He sighed. "Fine, but don't say you didn't ask for it. I stole my dad's friend's car once. I was high on God knows what, and I drove it into the side of a restaurant."

She covered her lips with her fingertips. "Oh my God. Was anyone..."

"No one was hurt. Luckily they were closed for repairs and there was minimal damage, but my dad was furious. Threatened to take me out of the will if I didn't get my shit together. And he was right to do it, too. But he lost a lot of business from that friend."

"What does your dad do, exactly?"

"Uh-uh," he said, waving a finger. "Don't think you're getting out of this so easily. Worst thing. Your turn."

She closed her eyes. "When I was seventeen, I ran away from home."

"What? Like, suitcase packed full of crackers and juice ran away from home or legitimately ran away?"

"My boyfriend and I tried to cross state lines with fake IDs to get married."

Asher's jaw dropped. "Did you?"

The corner of her mouth drew up into a grimace. "No. I chickened out. I didn't know what would happen if we got caught. But we were gone for three days. My parents called the police and everything."

"Wow," he said, staring over her shoulder as he took in what she was telling him. "I guess we both did some pretty fucked up shit."

"It *is* the teenage curse."

He nodded, standing up and lifting her hand into the

air, pulling her into his chest. "Enough about being teenagers, I have some very adult activities planned for us upstairs."

"Oh, you do, do you?" She smirked, lifting her chin so that her lips could brush his.

He let out a soft moan, rolling his head back before pulling her upstairs with passion in his eyes. There were three doors, but Asher didn't bother showing her around as he led her into the one on the right, shutting it behind them as he flipped on the light. There was a beautiful, king-size wooden bed against the far wall. Its headboard looked completely custom, and Blythe guessed it probably cost more than she would spend on her entire future house's furniture. It was covered with a white comforter and plush, decorative pillows.

Quieting her thoughts, his lips collided with hers, unbuttoning his dress shirt and loosening his belt. It wasn't the first time they'd been together, but for some reason everything about this time felt brand new. He pulled her shirt over her head, his hands cupping her head as he bit her bottom lip. His mouth moved to her neck, his tongue warm on her skin and the sound of his breath in her ear. He flipped off the light, laying her down in near-darkness, only a sliver of moonlight creeping through the curtains on the window. She laid in bed, waiting as she heard his shoes coming off, and then his pants.

In an instant, he was back on top of her, his mouth on her chest as his hands toyed with her skirt, trying to find the zipper on the side. When he located it, he pulled the zipper down with such force she half wondered if he'd broken it, but she couldn't bring herself to care as his fingers made their way to her panties.

He was naked on top of her, and she could feel his excitement for her against her thigh. He pulled the straps of her bra down, freeing up her breasts as he placed his mouth over them, one by one, taking his time as the moans escaped her throat involuntarily.

She moved to take her panties off, but he stopped her, lowering himself so that his mouth was over the fabric. She could feel his hot breath against her skin, her hips rising and falling as he teased her.

She tried again to remove them, but this time he pinned her hands down, keeping his mouth between her legs. When he spoke, his lips danced against her most sensitive area.

"Not yet, baby. You're all mine tonight." He kissed the fabric. "I'm all yours." *Kiss.* "And this night is *all* ours."

CHAPTER FIFTEEN

"One green tea and one iced coffee please," Blythe said, holding out the cash as the barista behind the silver street cart began to make the drinks. Blythe took a step back, watching as she worked while lost in thought.

It had been nearly two months since she'd met Asher's family, and in that time, they'd practically spent every free moment together. Asher had stuck to his word, making sure she knew how committed to her—and only her—he was. She was falling for him, as hard as that was to believe. New York had never been about finding love. And certainly not this quickly. Of course she'd wanted love. She wanted the fairy tale she'd always dreamed of, just like she told Finn, but things were—

"Blythe?" She spun around, looking for the source of the voice in her ear. There he was, as if conjured by the mere thought of him. She hadn't seen Finn in two months. Hadn't thought of him in...well, at least a few hours. But there he was. He was filthy, dressed in work boots, muddy clothes, and a hard hat. He slid the hat off, staring at her in disbelief. "W-what, what are you doing here?"

"I'm, um," she swallowed, taking the drinks from the barista as she held them out, "getting coffee."

"I can see that," he said. "Two."

She stepped out of the line of people, her breathing shallow as she waited for him to say something. Anything. "Mhm." Her face burned from his presence, her heart racing in her chest.

"So, I guess that means you two made up, huh?"

"What?"

"Two coffees," he said again, gesturing toward the cups in her hands.

"Oh." She shook her head to clear her jumbled thoughts. "Um, yeah. Yeah, we made up."

He swallowed and, try as she might to read his expression, she couldn't. He was stone. Unreadable. Or perhaps just emotionless. "That's good," he said finally.

"Are you…I mean, is everything good…with you?"

He nodded. "Yeah, everything's fine. Just got off work."

"I figured," she said, moving one cup-filled hand up and down slightly toward his attire.

"Right." A soft laugh escaped his throat, and she'd be lying if she said it didn't make her stomach twist into a knot. "Well, I'm glad it all worked out for you, then." He lifted his hat from his side slightly in a small salute. "I'll, uh, I'll be seeing you."

"Finn?" she asked before he could turn around.

"Yeah?" His eyes met hers, and they were softer somehow. Hopeful.

"Weren't you coming to get coffee?" she asked, pointing to the cart with her thumb.

He stared at it for a minute and then looked back to her. "No. Er, well, maybe. But...I'm just going to head home."

"Don't let me run you off," she said, her tone defensive. "I was just leaving."

He frowned. "You aren't running me off, Blythe. It was...it was really good to see you, actually."

"It was?"

"Yeah." The small smile on his face told her he meant it. But then why had he pushed her away? Why had he made her decision so easy? If he hadn't forced her to leave, there was a very real chance she would've never gone back to Asher. Not that she wasn't happy—she was. But could she be happier? She'd never know now.

"Well, it was good to see you, too."

"I'm glad everything worked out for you."

"Who says it did?" she asked.

"Didn't it?"

"Asher's a good guy," she told him. "He's made a really big effort to show me he's serious about us."

"You didn't answer my question." His mouth contorted in thought. "Are you happy?"

"Do you care?" she asked, her voice so soft that he had to lean in to hear her.

He was still for a moment. "I do. But I shouldn't."

"Because you're dangerous?"

"Because I put you in danger."

"I'm a big girl, Finn. I can take care of myself."

"You shouldn't have to. If this guy makes you happy, you should be with him."

She nodded. "Well, he does."

"Good."

Her lips squeezed into a thin line as she tried to think of what to say next. He was being stubborn. Difficult. He obviously had secrets. Asher was easy. Simple. Fun. And he cared about her. So, why couldn't she keep herself from hoping that Finn would keep talking? Why did she want more with a man who'd made it clear there was no future to be had with him?

"Okay, I'm going to go," he said finally, letting out a loud sigh. "I'll see you around."

"See you," she whispered, watching him walk out of sight. Her phone chimed in her pocket, breaking her trance, and she glanced down, knowing it would be Asher wondering where she was. With her hands full, she had no way of checking it, but she turned and walked back toward his apartment in a hurry. He was just leaving work and, with any luck, she was going to surprise him.

"HEY, STRANGER," Asher said, pulling her in for a kiss as soon as he saw her. He took his iced coffee from her hand. "I was hoping I'd get to see you tonight."

They walked up the stairs, hand in hand, as she took a sip of her drink. "Sorry," she told him. "I wanted to respond to your message, but it came through as soon as both of my hands were occupied."

He lowered his brow. "I didn't text you."

"You didn't?" she asked. "Well, I wonder who it was, then?" As they reached his floor, she pulled the phone from her pocket, turning it over so she could read the screen. "How was work?" she asked, before her eyes registered what she was seeing.

"You'll never guess who scored a brand new, million-dollar account," he said proudly, turning the key in his door and pushing it open so she could enter.

She stared at the screen, only half listening to what had been said. The text message was from Finn. He'd put his phone number in her phone the second night she stayed with him, and it had been in there tormenting her ever since. She teetered between texting him and deleting it completely just about every day.

It read, **Come by my place tonight. It won't take long. I'll be there until 8.**

What could he possibly want? And why didn't he just tell her to her face when she saw him? He'd been texting her as he walked away. Was that really easier than just talking to her?

"Hello? Are you listening?"

She jerked her head up. "Sorry, Asher. I'm sorry. What'd you say?"

The smile fell from his face. "Is everything okay?"

She exited out of the text message. "It's just...it's work."

"Do you need to go?"

She bit her lip. "I think so."

"What do you mean you think?"

As she slid the phone back into her pocket, she pulled

him in for a kiss. "I'm sorry. I do have to go. I'll try to come back, though."

He nodded skeptically. "Okay...well, thanks for the coffee, I guess. You're sure everything's okay?"

She smiled, trying to reassure him while hiding the worry from her own face. What did Finn want? What was he going to say to her? What did she want him to say? "Everything's fine," she promised.

"Okay, be careful. I love you," he said, walking further into the apartment.

She froze, his words slamming into her chest so hard they could've knocked her down. "What?"

He turned back around, his face ashen, jaw dropped open. "Oh my God. I...um...I didn't—shit. It just slipped out."

"You...you love me?" she asked, a lump rising in her throat. It had been so long since anyone had said those words to her. Did he mean them? Did she want him to?

He swallowed, running a thumb under his nose. "I..." A small smile crept onto his lips. "Yeah, Blythe, I do. I love you. I know it's fast. I mean, two months is...well, it's no time at all, but...I've never felt for anyone the way I feel about you. When I'm not with you, I'm thinking about you, and when I am with you, I'm thinking about how I never want you to leave."

Her jaw fell open and she sucked in a breath, suddenly unable to form words.

"You don't have to say it back," he whispered, his voice showing more vulnerability than she'd ever heard from him. "But I wanted you to know."

"Asher...I—"

"Go on to work," he told her, kissing her cheek. "I'll be here if you want to come back by."

"Are you sure?"

"Yeah, of course."

Her chest was tight as she turned to walk away, her emotions conflicted. She should stay. She should tell him that nothing is more important than the three words he just said to her, but she'd be lying to him—and herself—if she said she wasn't curious what Finn could want. And so, she walked down the stairs, listening to his door shut behind her and wondering if she was making the biggest mistake of her life.

TWENTY MINUTES LATER, she was climbing up the last flight of stairs toward Finn's apartment. Apprehension filled her gut, but she knew there was a small bit of hope in there, too. A bit of hope she was learning to hate with every passing step.

When she got to his door, it was cracked open. She hesitated, wondering for just a moment if it might be a trap, but without allowing herself to think too much, she pushed it open.

"Finn?" she called. As she entered the apartment, a gasp escaped her throat. It was empty. The couch, the TV, all of his furniture was gone. Had he been robbed? She turned around, her breath suddenly too loud in the silent apartment.

Footsteps approached her from behind and she spun toward the bedroom, letting out a sigh of relief.

"You came," he said. He'd changed out of his work clothes and cleaned up since she'd seen him last, though he still seemed to be sweating. In his hands was a box with a letter on top.

"What's going on?" she asked, gesturing toward the empty apartment in case he hadn't noticed.

"I'm moving," he said simply.

"Moving? Leaving New York?"

"I have some things I need to take care of." He set the box down on the countertop, lifting the envelope and turning it over in his hands.

"Will I ever see you again?" she asked. She hated the pain that filled her voice, but there was no hiding it.

"I…" He pinched the bridge of his nose, looking down and letting out a breath. "I don't think so. Here." He slid the envelope to her.

"What's this?" she asked, staring at the shaky hand-written '**Blythe**' on the front of it. She ran her fingers over the ink. His hands were on her arms before she realized it, and when she looked up, his lips found hers. She tensed up for a moment, thinking she should resist, but her body melted to his touch instantly. His kiss was soft, gentle, his lips warming her in ways she hadn't known possible. The world stood still. None of the confusion mattered. The empty apartment. The endless opportunities held within the envelope in her hands. The eminent heartbreak his leaving was sure to cause her. For just that split second, with her lips on his and his hands cradling her head, nothing else mattered. When the kiss ended, he pressed his forehead to hers.

"God, what I wouldn't do to kiss you forever," he whispered.

She sucked in a breath, feeling cool tears stinging her eyes as she realized how real it all was. Her feelings for him. The rush he sent from her fingers to her toes. And the fact that he was about to walk out of her life forever. "Don't go." It was a command. A plea. A promise.

His nose touched hers and, for just a moment, she thought he was going to give in, that his lips would find hers again and time would stop for them. She was wrong.

His hands left her head, and she heard his feet shuffle as she closed her eyes. "Finn, please…"

"Just…just read the letter," he whispered. "Take care of yourself, Blythe."

With that, the door clicked shut and hot, angry tears flooded her cheeks. *Damn it.* She ripped open the letter with force, furious thoughts radiating through her. She could still catch him. She could still stop him from leaving.

But could she? Would he listen? She had to find out what was in this all-important letter.

BLYTHE,

I did a search for the number you used to call your aunt from my phone, and this is the address it pulled up. I hope it's right.

It's Finn, by the way. If you hadn't figured that out. Guess that's where I should've started.

If you're wondering why I didn't just scrap this

letter and start all over, it's because this is my eighteenth attempt, and my hand is getting sore.

I should just text you, I know. Who writes letters anymore? Do you know how hard it was to even find a pen in my apartment?

There I go rambling again. I won't waste too much of your time.

I wanted to let you know that I'm moving. Leaving the city for a while to clear my head. I have some things I need to do, stuff I need to get taken care of, and...my head just isn't in the right place. It seems New York isn't big enough for the both of us.

Yeah...I really should just scrap this and start over, shouldn't I? Maybe I'll get lucky and this won't ever get to you. Then I'll just have wasted a bunch of money but save my dignity.

Money. Yeah, that's where I was going with this. You'll find a key in this envelope, too. I'm not including my address just in case this does happen to end up in the wrong hands, but if it doesn't, Blythe, if it ends up in your hands...the apartment is yours.

I've paid up the rent for a full year. Okay...technically eleven months by the time you get this. Do what you want with it. You deserve a fresh start, Blythe. If anyone can understand that, it's me. I've signed the lease over into your name, which you'll also find a copy of in this envelope. Use this start wisely. Save your money. Travel. Whatever you want to do. I hope this helps you in some way.

Stay safe. Take care of yourself. Don't think about me too much.

I'll say this now because I'll never have to see you again...I think maybe you changed me, Blythe. For the better. You made everything different. I was worried I would do the same for you, but in an opposite way. I'm not good for you. My life is dangerous. Don't look for me. I learned a long time ago how to disappear, and you won't find me. Trust me when I say it's for your own good.

You told me once that you wanted it all. The fairy tale. Well, I can't give you that, but consider this your pumpkin carriage. That's what Cinderella got, right? Something along those lines. This is yours.

I hope you get the full fairy tale.

~~Your friend~~

~~Your fairy god—wtf~~

The damn idiot who needs more sleep and is leaving you an apartment and isn't going to write any more,

Finn

SHE READ through the letter twice as tears continued to blur her vision. She laughed through parts and sobbed through others. The key and lease fell from the envelope when she turned it over, just like he'd said. She opened the lease, reading through it carefully. He had, in fact, signed it completely over to her. There was a yellow receipt stapled to the front that showed twelve months had been paid in full.

She turned the key over in her hand, rushing toward the window and looking out, wanting to see him walking away. Which direction would he go? Could she follow him? Should she?

She thought back to the letter. *I learned a long time ago how to disappear...*

He didn't want to be with her. She had a man who loved her waiting for her just a few blocks away. Finn didn't want her to find him. He'd made that incredibly clear. Finn planned to disappear. The only question... could he just as easily be erased from her heart?

CHAPTER SIXTEEN

"That's the last of the boxes," Asher said, setting it down on her couch with a loud groan. "And, thank God." He wiped his forehead dramatically. "You know they make movers for this kind of thing, right?"

"Why on earth would I need movers when I have such a handsome and strong boyfriend?" Blythe popped up from behind the sink, walking toward him with one hand on her hip. She patted his cheek playfully, kissing his lips. He ran a finger over the bandana headband tied around her ponytail.

"Fair enough," he said. "So, what room are we unpacking first?"

"I was thinking maybe the kitchen? Then I could whip us up something to eat while you put my bed together."

"Ah, an ulterior motive if I've ever heard one," he said, patting her bottom as she turned to walk away. "I didn't know you cooked."

She scoffed. "You do know I work for a caterer, don't you?"

He laughed, opening a bottle of water from the fridge and taking a drink. "Of course, I know that. I just didn't know it was something you really enjoyed. I thought it was...I don't know, just a job. You said you liked baking before, but not cooking."

"It is just a job, I guess," she told him. "Baking is my favorite, you're right. I actually do really love to cook, though. Since I moved to the city I haven't been able to do it for fun, but now that I have my own place, maybe I can start again."

"As long as I can be the taste tester."

"You have my word."

He grabbed her waist, spinning her around so that she was leaning up against the counter, his lips on her ear. "I think I have a better idea of what we can do first."

She giggled as his hands slid up her stomach, his fingertips tickling her skin. "Stop it!" she squealed. "If we don't get to work, we'll spend all day doing *that*, and I desperately need to get unpacked."

He pulled back, a giant grin on his face as his hands went up innocently. "Okay, okay," he teased. "Whatever you say."

She set a box up onto the counter, and they slowly began unpacking, being careful of the glass dishes she'd purchased with her most recent paycheck. She wished she had something of her parents' to make it feel like home, but nearly everything had been lost in the fire. She'd purchased a few candles that smelled of her mother's favorite scent and planned to burn them every chance she got. Truth be told, the apartment reminded her more of Finn than anyone, but with enough time, and enough memories made with Asher, she knew that would fade.

In the weeks since he'd disappeared, she'd gone from thinking about him constantly, to only thinking of him once or twice a day. It was progress. Besides that, Asher was everything that she wanted in a man. He was stable. Loving. Kind. He made her laugh. He made her feel safe. Anything she felt for Finn, however fleeting and over-whelming it had been, was pure lust. It would pass.

"Hey, I forgot to ask you. What are you doing for Thanksgiving?" Asher asked, interrupting her thoughts as he leaned across her to set a glass bowl into the cabinet.

"Oh, gosh, that's next month, isn't it? I don't have any plans. Why do you ask?"

"You have plans now," he said.

"Oh yeah? What kind of plans?" She leaned against the counter, watching him work.

"My parents have a huge dinner. More food than you could ever eat. And they asked that I invite you."

"To Thanksgiving dinner? I don't know," she said, wringing her fingers. "Isn't that a family thing?"

"You're part of our family."

"I know," she said, rolling her eyes playfully. "I mean, they all seemed to love me at the party. And what's not to love?" she joked. "But—"

"No buts," he said, pulling her to him. "They love you. As do I. And you're coming. It wouldn't be Thanksgiving without you there."

"Are you sure?" she asked, studying his face.

"I'm positive." He kissed her nose. "It's going to be great." He pulled away, grabbing another dish and stacking it in the cabinet carefully. She watched him, the man she'd grown so close to in such a short time. He'd invited her into his world, into his family. He'd taken care of her. Protected her. Loved her in a way that no one else ever had. Sure, their start hadn't been perfect, but he'd made up for it tenfold since then. He was good to her, and for the first time, she was realizing she didn't want to take advantage of that anymore.

"Asher?" she said, her voice wavering.

"Yeah?" he asked over his shoulder.

"I love you, too."

He froze, lowering the dish and turning around slowly. His brown eyes were wide with shock as they met hers. Without a word, his arms were back around her waist, lifting her up to sit on the countertop before he kissed her. His fingers tangled in her hair as his kiss grew more passionate, as if his mouth were searching for oxygen only hers could give.

"I love you so much," he told her. It had been a month since he'd said the words the first time, and never once had he pressured her to say them back, even though he'd said it a few times since then.

Her first experience with love in high school had been awkward and forced. They'd said 'I love you' between classes, in a note passed on the first day they'd become boyfriend-girlfriend. It was just what boys and girls did. They were fifteen and had no idea what love meant. With Asher, it was different. The feelings were real. The sentiment was there. Her heart fluttered at his touch, not because a teacher might catch them at any moment, but because he made her feel like no one else could. This was real love. The kind she'd spent her whole life dreaming about.

"I love you, too," she whispered as she felt cool tears filling her eyes again. The last time she'd cried in this apartment, it had been over a man who she knew hardly anything about. This time, it was because her heart was overflowing with emotion. Asher pulled away from her slightly, his breath warm on her face.

"That's the first time you've said that," he told her.

"Mhm."

"I was starting to think you just enjoyed torturing me."

She laughed softly. "Maybe just a little."

"Oh yeah?" he teased, lifting her up and carrying her down the hallway with heavy footsteps.

"Yeah."

"Maybe we need to make that bed first priority," he said, lifting his lips to find hers again as they reached the bedroom.

"Who needs a bed?"

CHAPTER SEVENTEEN

The week of Thanksgiving came quickly, though it was a month later. Blythe had requested the entire week off due to their out-of-town trip. Tony hadn't been happy about it, and she sensed that he was getting tired of her requests off even though she tried to keep them minimal. But he couldn't deny that she was one of the best workers he had when she was there.

If she lost her job, there would be others Asher had assured her. Better ones even. He had connections. Time and time again, he'd tried to get her to let him set her up at a restaurant, making double what she made as a caterer, and with a better schedule, too.

As much as she wanted to take the offer, she desperately wanted to hang onto the only piece of her life that still felt like hers. She was living in Finn's apartment. Her days were spent with Asher. Her childhood had relied heavily on her parents, friends, and boyfriend. Her job was the only thing she'd acquired on her own. She'd grown sentimental about that.

On Wednesday, Asher took her to the cabin, though this time it wouldn't be all theirs.

"My parents will stay at their house, but we'll have family in from all over, so all of the bedrooms in each of the cabins will be taken. Luckily, we still get the master in our cabin and most of the kids will be in the West cabin, so we shouldn't be bothered too much."

"Did I meet most of your family at Grandmother Lorene's birthday?"

He chuckled. "Not even close. My family is pretty big."

"Wow," she said. "You never told me that."

"I don't see most of them that often." His jaw went tight as he said it, and she sensed there must've been some tension there she didn't know about just yet.

She reached across the car, taking his hand as they pulled up to the cabins. "It's going to be okay. I'm excited to meet everyone. It just means I'll get to know you even more."

"Yeah," he agreed, though his voice was distant. When the car came to a stop, she looked around at the full driveway, loaded with luxury vehicles. Several men stood around talking and laughing while their wives wrangled kids and sipped on glasses of wine despite it being barely three o'clock.

"Asher!" one man called, and all heads turned their direction.

"Hey, everyone!"

"And this must be the lovely Blythe." The oldest of the bunch took her hand, kissing it lightly and then patting where his lips had been with his free hand. "Archibald Grace, Asher's great-uncle."

"It's nice to meet you," she said.

His eyes lit up, his face as animated as a kid at Christmas. "And listen to that Southern twang." He giggled along with the others.

"Easy, Archie," Asher warned, his voice a low growl. Blythe squeezed his arm.

"It's all right," she assured him. "Honestly, I'm used to it. Besides, y'all sound strange to me, too, so we're even."

Archie looked positively giddy as she spoke. "Your mother is absolutely thrilled about her, Ash. I can certainly see why."

Asher wrapped a proud arm around her shoulders. "She may be the one thing I do right by my parents," he said, and the others laughed, though Blythe couldn't help blushing at his comment. "Anyway, we're going to go settle in."

"Sounds good. You'd better call dibs on your room. I think a few of them are already full," a younger man she hadn't been introduced to yet said.

"Sounds good, Eric. Good to see you, man."

"Likewise," he called, waving a casual hand over his head as Asher threw their bags over his shoulder and turned to lead her toward the cabin.

"You weren't kidding about the big family," she said once they were out of earshot.

"You haven't met half of them yet," he whispered in her ear. When they reached the door, he let go of her shoulders, turning the knob and pushing it open to let her through. "Ladies first."

She stepped into the cabin, taking a look around. It hadn't been so long since she'd been there last, but this time the home looked incredibly different. The living room was filled with suitcases and bags, scattered shoes, scarves, coats, and purses.

"Excuse the mess," he told her. "I told you it would be crowded."

"I see that. Where is everyone?" she asked.

"Anyone home?" he called loudly, his voice echoing through the quiet house. "Most of them are probably out back or they've run to town for a bit. We'd better get these bags in our room before someone claims it."

"Well, I certainly hope they weren't napping," she teased, turning to head up the stairs. When the top floor came into view, she took a step back, convinced she must be seeing things. She clutched her chest, her tongue sticking to the roof of her mouth like glue as she opened her mouth. She couldn't form words to describe what she was seeing. There was *no way* it could be real. No way *he* could be real.

"Finn?" Asher cried, quickly bounding up the stairs past her with his hand held out. He pulled Finn into a hug, patting his back. "Holy shit, man, where have you been?" Finn looked equally shocked to see her. His dumbstruck expression in no way matched the joy on Asher's face. "I can't believe you're here. Dad didn't tell me you were coming!"

"Yeah," Finn said halfheartedly. "I've been staying here for a while." His gaze briefly made it to Asher before trailing back to Blythe.

"Sorry," Asher said, zipping down two steps to grab Blythe's hand and pull her up the rest of the way. "Finn, this is my girl, Blythe. Blythe, this is my best friend."

Blythe remained frozen, though now at the top of the stairs. "H-hi," she said, unsure of what to say. How to explain this messed up situation.

"Hi," Finn said. "I should've known when you said Asher...of course, of all the Ashers in New York City, it'd be this one."

"What are the chances?" she asked, her gaze locked with his as she tried desperately to comprehend the situation.

"Well, we never did have much luck."

"Wait, I'm missing something," Asher said, his voice breaking their eye contact. "You two know each other?" His hand darted back and forth between them.

"Yeah, you could say that," Blythe said softly. "He... um...well, I don't really know what to say."

"The apartment she's living in?" Finn asked. When Asher nodded, he went on, "It used to be mine."

"What do you mean? You two were, what, dating?"

"No," Blythe said, probably too quickly.

"Our timing was never right," Finn told him, though he was still looking at her. "But anyway, I'm really happy for you two." He looked back at Asher. "Really. And it's good to see you, man. I hear you finally got that office at Finer Things. Your dad's been keeping me up to date. He didn't mention her, though."

Asher nodded, obviously thrown off. "Yeah, I, um, I did. He didn't tell me you two were still in contact. I thought you'd fallen off the map."

"I just needed some space, you know?"

"Ten years is a long time," Asher said.

Finn reached for Asher, pulling him into another

quick hug and patting Blythe's shoulder. "Anyway, I've gotta run to town. It was great to see you, Ash. We'll catch up soon." As he rushed down the stairs, he turned one last time and met her eyes, but she forced herself to look away.

He'd walked away before, and he'd keep on doing it. She gripped Asher's hand firmly. "Come on, let's get our bags put away."

CHAPTER EIGHTEEN

Once they were in the room and the bags were set down, Blythe shut the door.

"So…how do you know Finn?" Asher asked. "Really."

She sat down on the edge of the bed, avoiding eye contact as she ran her hands over her thighs nervously. "When I moved to New York, Finn was the first person I met. I can't believe you know him."

"Yeah," he said softly, sitting down in the desk chair across from her. "Finn was my best friend growing up. I mean, I guess he still is. We were in the same grade and inseparable. But about ten years ago he disappeared, and today's the first time I've seen him since then."

"What do you mean he disappeared?" Blythe asked, cocking her head to the side in confusion.

"Literally…he *disappeared*. Like, he was here one day and then…gone. I tried calling and texting him, but his phone was disconnected."

"Why would he disappear?" She stared at her hands,

trying desperately to piece together what seemed to be Finn's biggest secret.

"I have no idea," Asher said. "I thought maybe he'd been recruited as a spy." When she looked up, she noticed the smirk on his face, telling her he was only joking. She would've been lying to say that wasn't one of the possibilities on her mind as well.

"I'm serious, Asher. Why would he be here? Why wouldn't he have told you he was home, but he told your parents?"

"My parents took care of Finn his whole life. He was like a second son to them. Honestly, it doesn't surprise me that he went to them when he resurfaced. And I can't say I'm surprised he didn't look me up right away. I'm sure he knew our reunion would be...awkward at best."

"That's a bit on the nose, isn't it?" Blythe teased.

"Were you two...a thing?" Asher asked hesitantly, and she knew the jealousy in his voice was only mildly being kept at bay.

"No," she said. "Like he said, our timing was never right. We went out a few times, I won't lie to you, but I'm not even sure they were even dates."

"But he left you his apartment."

"He said he had to clear his head."

Asher scoffed. "You'd think ten years would be long enough to do that." He paused, chewing nervously on his bottom lip. "Look, be honest with me, do I have anything to worry about with you two?"

She took a breath. She wasn't going to lie to him. He deserved to know the truth, if only she knew what that was. "When I found out you'd been seeing other people, I went to Finn. I don't even know how I ended up there, but I did." She twisted a finger in the palm of her hand, a nervous tic of hers. "And, for just a moment, I thought we might become something. When you came back to me, I told you I wasn't sure I could be exclusive." She took a deep breath, preparing herself for her next words. "That was because of Finn. Because I wasn't sure what either of us wanted."

"So, what are you saying?" he asked, his voice raised slightly.

She leaned forward, reaching for his hand. "I'm saying...there are feelings there. For me, at least. But I'm with you, Asher. The past months with you have been amazing. I've never been so happy. That's because of you." She patted his chest with her fingertips. "You don't have anything to worry about with Finn. Not anymore."

His eyes filled with relief as he pulled her into his chest. "I love you, you know that?"

"I love you, too," she told him, kissing him firmly on the lips.

He stood, pushing her backwards on the bed with their lips still together. His hands took hold of her arms, pinning them back as he trailed kisses across her lips and down her neck. "What would I ever do without you?" he whispered into her ear, his warm breath on her skin causing cold chills to cover her body.

He pulled back slightly, their noses still connected. As she stared into his warm, dark eyes, she wondered the same thing. "Lucky for us both, you'll never have to find out."

"I'm serious, Blythe." He kissed her in between

sentence fragments. "I am," *kiss*, "so happy with you." *Kiss.* "Like...I didn't even know this," *kiss*, "was possible."

She giggled. "You keep me pretty happy, too."

His gaze moved from her lips to her eyes, darting back and forth between each eye. "I'm so sorry I ever hurt you."

She sat up, lifting one leg over his lap. "Asher, we've talked about this. What you did—seeing other people— you don't have to apologize for it. It was a long time ago, and we were so new, it wasn't like you cheated on me. We hadn't set boundaries or rules yet."

"Yeah, but how could I have been so blind that I didn't see I had it all right in front of me?"

She rolled her eyes playfully. "Well, that one's all on you."

He kissed her cheek, brushing a piece of her hair out of the way. "I'm just glad I didn't ruin it."

"Me too," she told him. "We were both lucky you came to your senses in time."

"Yeah," he said softly. "Apparently *just* in time."

CHAPTER NINETEEN

Thanksgiving dinner at the Graces' was nothing short of spectacular. Like Grandmother Lorene's birthday party, no expense was spared. The Grace's estate was breathtaking. The mansion was nestled on a two-hundred-acre maple farm, and the home alone was nearly eleven thousand square feet. With eight bedrooms and seven bathrooms, Blythe had to wonder why the family even bothered having three cabins for their guests to stay in. With a bit of effort, it would be entirely possible to have guests in the house you never had to see.

The dining room housed a one-hundred-and-twenty-five-foot-long table and, as Blythe and Asher arrived, the staff was busy setting it with a feast that could have adorned the cover of any holiday magazine.

"There she is!" Mona screeched, scurrying across the expansive entryway when she spied the couple. She pulled Blythe into a hug before turning to Asher and hugging him as well. "I'm so glad you could make it. I was hoping you wouldn't already have plans with your family."

"Mom, I told you Blythe's parents passed away," Asher said, his voice filled with contempt.

Mona's face went pale. "I'm so sorry, Blythe. He did tell me. I'd just forgotten."

"It's okay," Blythe assured her. "Thank you for inviting me."

"Oh, we wouldn't have it any other way," she said, appearing relieved. "Asher, did you see the special guest your father had at the cabins for you?" She wiggled her eyebrows playfully.

Asher looked confused for a moment before he nodded. "Finn?" His voice sounded much less enthused than it had yesterday at the mention of his best friend's name, and Blythe couldn't help worrying whether she'd caused irreparable harm to their friendship.

"Mhm," she said gleefully, either intentionally ignoring or just not noticing her son's lack of enthusiasm. "He's out back with your father now. I'm sure he'd love to meet Blythe."

Asher frowned. "Sure. Maybe later, Mom. Is there anything we can help with?"

"I don't think so," she told him. "Dinner is just about ready. We're waiting on Martin and Sharon to arrive. Then we'll be all set to eat."

A member of their staff approached them suddenly, stealing Mona's attention, and she hurried off after them and left Asher and Blythe alone in the doorway.

"Your home is immaculate," Blythe told him. "I can't believe you grew up here."

Asher nodded. "Yeah, well, it's nothing special."

"Are you kidding me? My house was one of the biggest

in Darlington, but it didn't even compare to half of this place. Not to mention the furniture in one room costs as much as our whole house."

He wrapped an arm around her. "I wish I could've seen it."

"Me too," she agreed sadly. It was one of the things that crossed her mind frequently as she and Asher grew closer. He would never know that side of her. Never meet her parents. Never see the bedroom she'd meticulously decorated as a teenager. It was all gone. Half of her life had gone up in a cloud of smoke, and sometimes she wasn't sure what to do with the rest of it. Most people, when they met someone new, introduced them to their past. Her past was just that, the past, forever. She had no plans to ever return to Darlington.

"Do you want a tour?" he asked. "Or I could take you outside, see some of the land. It's really beautiful out there."

"I'd like that a lot. Shouldn't we stay inside if dinner will start soon?"

"No one's in any hurry," he promised her.

As if on cue, the front door swung open and two strangers stood behind them. Asher greeted them, quickly introducing Blythe to his cousins and following them into the kitchen, promising to show her the grounds after dinner.

As the dining room began to fill with people—some faces she remembered, most not—Mona directed Blythe to the chair next to hers as Jacob gave a quick toast, thanking their guests both new and old and asking everyone to dig in.

Blythe's body burned, her skin on fire with adrenaline as she remained consciously aware of Finn sitting just a few seats away. He seemed to be equally aware of her, his gaze trailing to her and then away from her every few minutes. He spoke to the family comfortably, obviously familiar with everyone.

As dinner wound down, Asher set back in his seat, sliding his hand under the table and onto Blythe's thigh. She offered him a small smile before turning to Mona, who was rambling on about the Christmas shopping she was nearly done with.

"Dinner was wonderful, Mona," she said politely, wiping the corners of her mouth with her cloth napkin.

"Thank you, dear," she said. "I'm glad you enjoyed it. I certainly hope you've left room for dessert."

"I was hoping to show Blythe around for a bit, Mom. We'll come back in to grab some dessert later."

His mother's smile wavered just a bit, but she eventually agreed. "Make sure to show her the view from off the deck," she said. "No one should live without being able to see that once in their lifetime." Without another word, she turned to the woman next to her, a stout, pretty young thing named Annie, and began talking about the two-year-old alongside her.

With that, Asher stood up, pulling Blythe's arm carefully so she would stand as well. Blythe felt uncomfortable leaving the table while everyone else was still there, most done with their dinner, but still lingering to talk. Finn's eyes fell on her, his mouth slightly opened as he watched her leave the table. She wanted desperately to talk to him. To have a few minutes alone to discuss everything on her mind, but she knew that opportunity wouldn't present itself in this situation. Finn had to be forgotten. Asher was priority.

He led her out the back door and onto the large, covered back balcony. It overlooked the acres of woods in the valley below. Mona was right, the view was to die for.

"This is incredible."

"Can I be honest with you about something?" Asher blurted out, his voice rushed, stressed. It was obvious he'd been holding it in for a while.

She glanced over at him, at the way his forehead held a wrinkle of stress she wasn't used to seeing on his usually calm face. "Of course. What is it?"

"I...I'm not a jealous person, Blythe. I'm honestly not. I've always been the one with most of the power in relationships, and I've always made sure they weren't exclusive for this exact reason." He paused. "I don't want to get hurt."

"What are you talking about?"

"I'm not comfortable being around Finn anymore. I mean, the guy was my best friend. I used to know everything about him. But I don't now. I don't know hardly anything...except that you like him. *Liked*, maybe. But he likes you...present tense."

"What are you saying, Asher? Has he said something to you?"

"He doesn't have to. He hardly kept his eyes off of you all through dinner."

"I think that's a bit of an exaggeration, but even if it isn't, I can't help it if he was staring. I wasn't staring back."

"I know," he said, and she let out a small breath of

relief. "It's just...why did it have to be him, ya know? I can handle a bit of competition, but my best friend?"

"I don't want to cause any trouble between you two, Asher, believe me. If I'd known..."

"What?" he asked when she didn't finish her sentence. "If you'd known...what?"

"I don't know. I met Finn first. If I'd known you two were best friends, maybe I wouldn't have allowed myself to fall in love with you...but I did. And I wouldn't wish a life without you on myself. Truth is, Asher, as much as I wish this had happened any other way, I wouldn't want to change the outcome. I love you so much."

"I love you, too," he told her. "I can't stand the thought of losing you. I guess that's all I'm really trying to say. Everytime I see him staring at you, I get this sick feeling in my stomach. Jealousy. Rage. I think I'm starting to hate him, and that's not fair to anyone."

"I don't want to cause you to lose your best friend."

He took her hand. "Finn was my best friend, that's true, but I think..." His lips brushed her cheek. "I think you're my best friend now."

She ran her fingers over where his lips had been, her eyes filling with tears. "I am?"

"You're who I want to tell everything to, Blythe. You're the one I want to share everything with. I just love you so damn much it hurts."

She pulled him into a hug, her heart filled with so much joy it felt as if it were going to explode. She'd never felt that way. She'd never loved someone so deeply. "I love you, too, Asher. So much."

When they pulled apart, Asher tucked a piece of hair

behind her ear. "Good, because there's something I have to tell you."

"What's that?"

He took a deep breath, looking out across the sky before his gaze fell back to her. "I lied to you."

"Lied? About what?"

"I do know where Finn was. I'm not supposed to, but I do."

"We don't have to talk about him," she assured him, running a hand over his bicep.

"I know that. I just...I want you to know the truth about him. About why he left. Why he disappeared for ten years. You deserve to know how dangerous he is."

"Dangerous?" she asked, swallowing. She blinked her eyes rapidly. "What do you mean 'dangerous'?"

He closed his eyes as if bracing himself for a blow. "I wasn't supposed to know. My dad hired a lawyer for him, and I overheard them talking one day. My dad assured me it was nothing to worry about. He said he was going to get it taken care of, but after a few months went by and I still hadn't heard from Finn, I asked my dad again. He said Finn had gone away to clear his head. He said he needed space. But...I Googled him. I found out the truth."

"I don't understand. What are you saying?"

"He's saying I was in prison," the voice came from her right. She looked toward it, surprised to see Finn approaching them from inside. His lips were pressed into a thin line. "And he's telling you the truth. Like I should have all along."

CHAPTER TWENTY

They all stood frozen, looking back and forth at each other, waiting for someone to make a move.

"I'm sorry. I shouldn't have interrupted," Finn said softly. "Your dad wanted his jacket." He pointed to the blazer draped over the railing as he strolled across the deck and grabbed it.

"Wait, Finn—" Asher called, as his friend disappeared into the house. He looked back at Blythe with a sad expression. "I have to go talk to him."

"Go," Blythe said, encouraging him with her words, though what she really meant was 'Stay. Tell me everything.' She watched as Asher did as he was told, going after Finn with haste. Her throat was dry as she swallowed the lump that filled it. What was she doing here? What was the plan? How could she possibly last another night in the cabin just feet away from Finn while lying next to Asher? She wasn't sure she could survive it.

After a few moments, Asher returned, his head hanging down.

"How did it go?" she asked with a grimace. The look on his face told her it hadn't gone well.

He looked up, running a hand over his hair. "I don't know what to do."

"What do you mean?"

"He says he's not mad, but of course, he is. I'm a horrible best friend."

She approached him carefully, soothing him with her voice. "Hey, you are *not* horrible. You didn't know. None of us knew. And, Ash, it doesn't matter. Finn doesn't have a claim over me." It was partially true, at least. "You did nothing wrong."

"But I shouldn't have told you about him going to prison. That wasn't my place and, selfishly, I did it just to make sure you'd choose me." He stared at her with sorrow-filled eyes. "I don't want to be that person."

She pulled him into a hug. "I already chose you, Ash."

"He looks at you like…" He paused, looking down and then back up at her.

"Like what?" she asked, lowering her gaze.

"Like he wants to rip your clothes off," he said finally, catching her by surprise.

"Asher, Finn and I never—it wasn't like that between us."

"It wasn't?"

"No. It wasn't." She kissed his lips firmly. "I love you so much. So if you need to spend the weekend repairing your friendship, you can do that. I'll be right here."

He sucked in a breath. "He never even let me know that he was out. That he was back. My dad knew, but no one thought to mention it to me."

135

"Sounds like the bad friend in this relationship isn't you."

He nodded. "You're right. If he doesn't want to be around me, then that's fine. I've lived ten years without the man who used to be like my brother. I won't beg him to be in my life."

She lifted up on her toes, rubbing his cheek. "It's his loss."

He smiled at her, his spirits visibly lifting, and her heart warmed. She'd done what was necessary. Making Asher feel better was all that mattered to her. That was her place—standing by his side. Wherever Finn was, whatever he had done, it didn't concern her. Asher was the man of her dreams, her true happily-ever-after, and she had to force herself to stop thinking about the man who'd once consumed all of her thoughts.

BLYTHE AWOKE in the dark bedroom, her eyes heavy with sleep. She reached her arm across the bed, sitting up when her skin didn't connect with his. She looked around the room, her suspicions confirmed. Asher was gone.

"Asher?" she called, her voice echoing through the quiet room. She lifted the cover from her legs, her feet sliding quickly to the cold hardwood floor. The room was completely dark except for a sliver of moonlight coming in from the window to her right. She tiptoed across the room, trying to be as quiet as possible so as not to wake the other guests sleeping in the house. Or, she guessed she was the true guest. The others were family, except for Finn.

She opened the door slowly, thankful it didn't squeak like the rusty hinges of the farmhouse doors she'd grown up with. There was no sneaking to be done around that house. She'd always believed her father refused to apply WD-40 specifically so her parents would always know if she tried to sneak out. It had worked, she supposed. The squealing door had kept her honest.

She looked at the door to the bathroom, the yellow light shining out from under the wood, and heaved a sigh of relief. He must've woken her when he left to use the bathroom. She turned around to go back toward their room when she heard the water shut off and, within a second, the door was opening.

"Blythe?"

She expected to see Asher, but she knew the voice wasn't his. "Finn?"

"What are you doing?" they asked each other at the same time.

He ran a quick hand through his hair. "Listen, about earlier…"

She cocked her head to the side, waiting for him to explain. What possible explanation was there for the lie he'd told her? While, technically, she guessed there wasn't really a lie—it wasn't as if she'd come out and asked him if he was a criminal—it was a lie of omission all the same. "Why didn't you just tell me?" she asked, keeping her voice low.

He blew air from his nose, obviously trying to figure out what to say. Finally, he nudged his head in the direction of his bedroom. "Come with me, okay? Not out here." He started to walk toward the room but stopped when he noticed she wasn't following him.

She bit her lip, looking down the staircase. What would Asher do? He certainly wouldn't be okay with her following Finn into his bedroom. But it wasn't as if something was going to happen. She wouldn't let it. She meant every word she'd said to Asher. She loved him. But she needed to know the truth.

"Asher's gone," Finn said finally, interrupting her thoughts.

She glared at him. "Gone? Gone where?"

"He headed out a while ago. Said there was something he needed to do."

"He *talked* to you? Why wouldn't he tell me?"

He shrugged. "I overheard him telling someone downstairs. It sounded like he was on the phone. He didn't leave you a note?"

She shook her head, but truth be told, she had no idea. She hadn't been looking for a note—she'd been looking for a person.

"Go call him if you want," he gestured toward their bedroom, "but if you want to know about me...I'll be in my room. The choice is yours."

She nodded, watching him disappear into his bedroom, true to his word. As she stood, contemplating her next move and chewing her bottom lip, her stomach rumbled. Whatever choice she made would be wrong. She wanted to call Asher, wanted to know where he was and what he was doing. But the mystery surrounding Finn also had her dying to know the truth. If Asher came back now, there was a chance she'd never know. If she found out the truth from Finn, she could call Asher as soon as she was done.

Without allowing herself to debate any longer, she stepped forward, turning the knob to Finn's door and stepping inside. The room was almost identical to theirs except for the fact that Finn had his curtains pulled open, giving a perfect view of the mountains and an even better view of the man sitting on the edge of his bed. The disheveled T-shirt, the loose sweatpants, his messy hair. It all reminded her of the mornings they'd woken up next to each other. The room smelled of him—like soap mixed with his warm cologne. She took a breath, breathing in his scent. It was intoxicating.

She shook her head as if to clear him from her brain. "So?" she said angrily. "Speak."

He sighed, remaining seated on the edge of his bed. He didn't look even a bit surprised to see her standing in his doorway. "I should've told you," he admitted.

"Well, that's the understatement of the year. I was staying with a criminal, Finn. Is that who that man was? One of your criminal buddies? Did you really put me in danger?"

He stood up, half of his face hidden in the shadows cast by the moonlight. "Now, hang on just a second. You can be mad at me all you want. I wish that I'd told you, I do. But the minute I had even a hint that being with me might put you in any danger, I left. I told you I wasn't a safe choice. I told you I didn't belong in your life. So, you can be mad at me for not telling you the truth about my past, but you don't get to blame me for not considering your safety. That's *all* I've thought about. And I've made sure that you're safe. I've taken care of you. I gave you an apartment. I protected you."

"Is that what this is about? Because you gave me your apartment, now I owe you?"

He scowled. "When the hell did I say anything about you owing me anything, Blythe? I did what I did because I wanted to. Not for any other reason. I honestly had no intention of ever seeing you again. And, really, can you blame me for not telling you about my history? It's not exactly how I like to lead into conversations."

"You still should've told me."

"It's not just a box you check on a fucking job application, Blythe. Don't you understand that? This thing follows me everywhere I go. If I had to introduce myself by telling everyone I meet what I've done...no one would want anything to do with me. You included."

"What did you do, Finn? What were you in prison for?"

He closed his eyes, standing up from the bed finally. "If I tell you the truth...you'll never look at me the same."

"It can't be any worse than what I'm already imagining."

"Yes. I promise you it can."

"What did you do, Finn? You promised you'd tell me if I came in here. I'm here. So talk."

"I'm not a bad person."

"What did you do?" she repeated through gritted teeth. When he didn't respond, she reached for the door. "This was a waste of ti—"

"Murder." He spit the word out, reaching for her arm. "I went to jail for murder."

Her blood ran cold, and she turned around. Whatever she was imagining, he was right, this was worse. "W-what?"

"I'm so sorry I didn't tell you. It was ten years ago. I was a kid. A stupid kid who made a stupid mistake. It's taken everything from me, but I don't want it to take you, too."

"Finn…" she whispered, backing away from him. "How…how could you?" As he reached for her, she couldn't help seeing bloodstains on his hands, searching his eyes for the heartless killer that must be lying just below the surface.

"You don't understand. It's complicated. So much about my life has changed from who I was back then. I'm not who I was."

"You killed someone."

He pressed his lips together. "I'm still the same person you met on your first day in New York."

"No," she repeated, her voice filled with sudden fury. "No, you aren't. As far as I'm concerned, I wish we'd never met." She grabbed hold of the door handle, pulling it open. His hand met the wood, slamming it shut, his eyes burning into hers.

"You don't mean that," he challenged her.

"You don't know what I mean."

"I know you have feelings for me, Blythe. I know you wanted me before you knew the truth. I was an idiot for running away. I should've told you everything, should've fought for a real chance with you." He took a gentle hold of her arm.

"I'm with Asher," she said firmly. "You lost whatever chance you may have had. I don't want you anymore, Finn. I love him."

Her words stung him, she could see it in his eyes. He released her arm instantly. "Okay," he said finally, his jaw hanging open. "Just...if you change your mind, if you want to know more—"

"I won't," she told him, pulling the door open with force though he'd already released it, and rushed down the hall. Her heart was pounding as she closed her bedroom door, resting her back against it and letting out a heavy breath.

CHAPTER TWENTY-ONE

The next morning, Blythe sat on the edge of the bed, her stomach turning circles as she scrolled through her phone. How on earth had she once felt so safe around a man who'd done such horrible things? How had he managed to keep that part of himself from her so effortlessly? She supposed that's what criminals did, after all.

She'd told Asher she had an upset stomach, using the excuse to spend the morning searching the internet to find more details about Finn's past. He'd told her the truth, as multiple articles confirmed. At age seventeen, Finn O'Brien had committed murder in the second-degree. A drug deal gone bad had resulted in a forty-two-year-old man, Cedric "Ed" Jackson, being found the next morning with his skull crushed, the result of blunt force trauma. His head had been beaten against a building in an alley so hard he died instantly. Reports said no one had seen the assault, but two witnesses saw Finn entering the alley just before the attack. Finn was brought in for questioning less than a week later, and he confessed almost immediately. He claimed his dealer had been trying to assault him for money he didn't have and his actions had been done in self-defense. All in all, it was a terrible accident. With the *help* of his lawyer, he received ten years.

The articles contained pictures of the victim as well as a mugshot of Finn, his hollow eyes familiar but empty and distant. He was skinnier, a sign of the drug use. His face was dirty, his hands dirtier. He had the same hairstyle, but the similarities ended there. His words echoed in her head: *I'm not who I was.*

"Hey." Asher's voice called her back to reality from across the room. He'd popped his head in the doorway, staring at her with a bright smile. "How are you feeling?"

"I'm better," she lied, rubbing her belly. "I'm sorry this has been a lousy last day of vacation. I hope your mom understands."

"Of course," he told her, walking into the room and sitting next to her on the bed with a kiss on her forehead. She closed out of the browser before he could see what she'd been researching. "Everyone understands. I just feel so bad that you're sick."

"Oh, I think it was just a bit of heartburn, maybe. I'm feeling much better already."

His eyes lit up. "Are you sure?"

"Mhm," she assured him. "Positive."

He took her hand in his, leaning in and kissing her lips carefully. "I'm so glad."

"Me too," she told him, resting her head against his.

"I'm going to load up the car. You ready to head out?"

"I am." She nodded.

"Great, I've already gotten everything packed up. I'll

just grab your bag over here." He stood up, lifting her bag from the floor and looking around the room to make sure they weren't forgetting anything. "You packed your phone charger already?"

"It's in there."

"Okay. I think that's everything, then." He held out a hand to her. "Ready?"

"Ready," she confirmed, taking his hand and slipping the phone into her pocket. He kissed her fingers, leading her out of the bedroom and down the stairs. As the living room came into view, Blythe immediately knew something strange was going on. The cabin's living room was full of people, all of the family gathered around with flutes of champagne in their hands. No one seemed to be talking, all eyes on them as they descended the staircase.

Mona rushed forward, surprising Blythe by pulling her into a quick hug. "I'm so sorry that you've fallen ill, dear."

"Oh, I'm okay. Just a bit queasy. Honestly, it's probably just from eating too much yesterday. I couldn't help it with all of the amazing food."

Mona patted her chest humbly, though she was obviously proud, pressing her lips into a firm smile as she looked away. "Oh, psssh." She waved off the praise but smiled again. "Thank you."

"What is everyone doing here?" Blythe asked finally, staring around the quiet room.

"One last tradition before we hit the road," Asher explained, taking a glass from a table in the corner and handing it to her. He took another for himself, drinking it quickly.

"Drinking is your family tradition before hitting the road?" Blythe asked, a small smirk on her face. "That seems...appropriate."

"Just a glass," Asher told her. "It's more for nerves than anything."

"Nerves?"

He looked to his mother, who squeezed Blythe's arm before making her way back to stand beside Jacob. "Sixty years ago, my grandfather proposed to my Grandmother Lorene, right here, on the Friday after Thanksgiving. Nearly every year since then, someone's made a huge announcement on this day, right before we leave. My dad proposed to my mom here thirty years ago."

"Steve proposed to me there six years ago," a woman in the back told her, raising her glass. Blythe couldn't seem to recall her name.

"We announced this little guy in that spot last year," another woman said, holding up the baby in her arms. Blythe was pretty sure the baby was called Declan, but she hadn't spoken to the mother much since they arrived.

"So, it's kind of an anniversary of sorts, this day, for most of us," Asher told her, running a hand down her forearm. She took a sip of her wine.

"That's sweet," Blythe said, staring around the room at the large family. Despite her perception of rich New York families, everyone in this room had been nothing but warm and welcoming to her. Asher's family was truly special. And happy. Happiness seemed to follow them everywhere.

Asher turned to her then, and Blythe's stomach dropped, seeing the anxious look on his face. It wasn't possible. There was no way he was about to...*and there he goes.* Down on one knee.

"Blythe, I..." Her heart thudded so loudly in her chest she could hardly hear him. Her face grew hot as she tried to focus and forget about the fact that every eye in the room was on her. Strangers. Asher's family. People who were counting on her to say 'yes.' Yes to a life with a man that she loved. Because...she did love him. There was no doubt in her mind. She loved Asher. But was she ready for this? For a lifetime together?

It seemed too soon. But wasn't this exactly what she'd told Finn she wanted just six months ago? A fairy tale. A happily ever after. And Asher was willing to give that to her. To take care of her.

Focus.

"I know this is soon. I do. But I love you, Blythe. I love you more than anything else in this life. I never thought I'd want to settle down before I turned thirty...but it doesn't feel like settling with you. It feels like getting everything I've ever wanted. It feels perfect." She smiled at him, feeling cool tears stinging her eyes at his words. It did feel perfect. It had for so long. The only thing making her doubt that now...was the man walking down the stairs.

She looked over, watching as Finn came down the stairs beside them. He was obviously the only one in the house not made aware of this plan. His mouth hung open for a moment and he stopped walking. He closed his mouth quickly, meeting her eyes as he watched the scene unfold in front of him. Asher was still talking, but she couldn't hear him. Was Finn going to fight for her? Would he say something? He didn't move, but no words left his mouth.

"And, I guess what I'm trying to say is, I want this. With you. I want all of it. A future. A white picket fence. A family. I want to wake up every day next to you and kiss you goodnight before bed. I don't ever want to wonder 'what if?' or 'what could've been?' You mean everything to me and, as much as I thought I wanted to wait, I don't want that anymore. I don't want you to ever question what you mean to me or where this is headed." He kissed her hands, reached into his pocket, and pulled out a small, black box. "So...what do you say? Will you marry me?" He opened it, and her mouth dropped open. It was a silver band with tiny diamonds creating an intricate, vintage design across the top and sides.

"It's beautiful..." she whispered.

"It was Grandmother Lorene's," he told her. "I snuck out and had it cleaned last night. I wanted it to be a surprise."

Tears continued to fill her eyes as she looked across the room to where Grandmother Lorene sat next to Mona. The two women had fat tears in their kind eyes. They loved her as much as she could ever hope a mother- and grandmother-in-law would love her. Asher was saying everything she'd wanted to hear. His proposal was everything she could've wanted. She smiled at him, though she couldn't help looking up one last time to where Finn stood.

He nodded slowly, his expression grim, and turned around, walking back up the stairs before he heard her answer. She looked back down at Asher, her decision made.

He raised his brow. "You aren't going to make me stay down here forever, are you?" He laughed nervously.

She giggled, covering her mouth with her free hand. "No," she said, placing her hands around the sides of his face. She bent down, placing a soft kiss on his lips. "Yes. Yes, Asher, I'll marry you."

Cheers were heard all around. Asher stood, scooping her up and spinning around in a circle, their lips pressed together despite the laughs escaping from both of their throats.

"I love you," he whispered, his voice so low that only she could hear. It felt intimate, even with the eruption of noise around them.

"I love you, too," she vowed.

"Forever." He set her down, pulling the ring out of its box and sliding it onto her shaking finger, her hand trembling. It wasn't a perfect fit, it needed to be loosened a bit, but it looked gorgeous on her finger. It was a sight she'd waited for her entire life. Her future lay in front of her, and as she looked into his eyes, she was sure the decision she'd made, the life she'd chosen, was right.

CHAPTER TWENTY-TWO

THREE MONTHS LATER

Blythe brushed a loose piece of hair back into her ponytail, her forehead covered in sweat. She sat down onto the couch, blowing air up over her face from her bottom lip. A knock on the door startled her. Why would Asher be knocking?

She stood, walking over to the door and looking through the peephole. His face caused her to gasp.

"Hey," he said, obviously able to hear her through the door.

She pulled it open without a second thought. What was he doing there? "Finn?"

He nodded. "Is this a bad time?"

"No," she stepped back, allowing him to enter the apartment, "not at all. What's going on?" She closed the door behind him, watching as he took in the changes she'd made. The once-bare walls now boasted art and the old, mostly empty living room was filled with a couch, two chairs, and plenty of throw pillows.

"The place looks…nice."

"Thanks," she said, trying not to grimace about the mess. In the far corner of the living room sat a pile of boxes, and there another box on the counter. Evidence that she was planning to move again. "Is everything okay?"

He nodded. "I…um, sorry to just drop by unannounced. Martin notified me that you were vacating the apartment." His words were formal, his voice monotonous; either he didn't care one bit, or he was doing a damn good job of hiding how much he cared.

"Yeah," she said, tapping one foot behind the other. "I, um, well, I'm moving in with Asher after the wedding in four months. I went ahead and let him know since it will be before the lease ends."

He blinked, nodding his head.

"I mean…thank you. For the apartment. You really saved me when I needed it most—"

He looked down, smiling sadly with a scoff. "It's no big deal."

"It was, Finn. It was a big deal."

His gaze trailed up her body, causing a cold chill to dance across her skin. When his dark eyes met hers, she sucked in a breath. "Well, look," he said finally, "if you're going to move out, I'll take the apartment back."

"Right," she said, his words catching her off guard. "Right, of course. Yes, definitely. I'd hate for you to have wasted your money."

"I don't care about the money, Blythe."

"What do you care about, then?"

He paused, seeming to think about it. "Are you happy?" he asked finally.

She thought about it—about the past several months with Asher, about the nights that he'd rubbed her head when she had a headache or her feet when she'd had a long day, about the walks through Central Park, the late night movies and ice cream, the way he kissed her, the way he could make her whole body set on fire with just a touch. "Asher is a really good guy," she told him. "He's good to me."

"That's not what I asked you."

"What are you asking, then? And why?"

"I'm asking if he makes you happy. If he's...*the one,* or whatever." He rolled his eyes. "I'm asking if you're settling."

"I'm not settling," she said quickly. "I'm happy."

He gave her a sharp nod. "Well, look at that. Less than a year in New York and you've got your fairy tale after all. I guess that's why people say it's the place where all your dreams can come true."

"Another nickname? I still say it's The Big Apple."

His eyes filled with passion, his expression growing serious. "That makes sense, too."

"What do you me—"

"It's filled with temptation."

She swallowed, her throat suddenly too dry. "Are you...um, are you planning to come to the wedding? We sent your save the date to his parents' house since we aren't sure where you're living."

"Sorry, yeah, I don't think I'm going to be making it."

She bit her lip, giving a slow nod. "Asher will be disappointed to hear that."

"I just think it's best if I stay away."

"You don't have to do that."

"Trust me, I do."

"Okay," she said finally. "Well, I'll get the keys to you as soon as I move out. And...thank you again. I can't tell you how much this," she gestured to the apartment around her, "meant to me. How much it still does."

"Apparently not enough," he whispered, not moving.

"What does that mean?"

He scowled. "You know what it means, Blythe."

"What do you want from me, Finn? What am I supposed to do?"

"Nothing," he said firmly. "As long as you're happy. Though something tells me you aren't."

"Why do you think that?" She tried to seem more sure of herself than she felt. She didn't know what it was about Finn that made her feel so nervous. Her feelings for him were fading—they had to be. She loved Asher, but she couldn't deny the hold Finn had over her. They were connected somehow. It had started the moment she met him, and no matter what she did, she couldn't seem to break that link.

"Because I know you, Blythe. I know what happiness looks like in your eyes. I know the way you move when you're happy. You're lighter. You were lighter with me."

"I never got a chance to *be* with you, Finn. You made that choice. Asher chose me." She pointed to her chest, her anger growing. "He chose me when you walked away."

"For your own protection," he insisted. Then he sighed, rubbing his hand over his hair. "I know now that I made a mistake. I should've stayed. I'd do anything to take it back."

"It doesn't work like that," she said, surprising herself when tears suddenly formed in her eyes. "You really hurt me when you walked away. I told you I wanted a chance with you. I wanted you to be an option."

"I still am!"

"You aren't," she said firmly. "I'm in love with Asher now."

"So you don't have feelings for me anymore?"

She squeezed her eyes shut, running a hand over her forehead. "I don't—"

"Be honest."

"Of course I have feelings for you, Finn. Only God knows why, but I do. But I have feelings for Asher, too. And we're engaged. This is just...it's too complicated."

"So, you're just going to take the easy road?"

"Isn't that what you did when you walked away?"

He scoffed, looking at the door with an open mouth. "Is that what you think? You think *anything* about that decision was easy?" He stepped closer to her, running his tongue over his lips. His eyes searched hers. "Blythe, that was the hardest thing I've *ever* had to do. Walking away from you that day, leaving you the note, knowing I'd never see you again...it destroyed me. Broke my heart. I've never felt toward anyone else the way I feel about you. Not even close. I...I think I'm in love with you."

She sniffled, the truth of his statement there in his eyes. "Finn..."

"I know," he said sadly. "I know this is the worst possible time, and I know I'm making your life more complicated. I get it. Honestly, I do. But I'm in love with you, Blythe. I think I may have been from the moment I met you." He lifted his hand to cup her cheek. She should've pulled away, but she couldn't move. "And if you can tell me you don't feel the same way, I'll let you go. I don't know how, but I will. *Only* if you can tell me you don't feel that way about me. That you don't think we at least deserve a chance."

His eyes darted back and forth between hers, waiting for her to say something, to make a decision. Her mind was a completely blank slate, the lie on the end of her tongue. She was prepared to say it. To tell him that she was over him. That she loved Asher and only Asher. That she didn't want to see Finn ever again.

Before she could make herself spit out the lie that would break her heart in two, his eyes darted in between hers one last time before falling toward her lips, and then his mouth was on her mouth, his lips pressed to her lips. He slid his hand back from her cheek to her hair, his fingers tangled in her dark brown locks.

Passion filled her stomach, her skin on fire as she fell into the kiss that felt more right than anything in her life. His other hand cradled the opposite side of her face, her body melting into him. Everything he said was right, every word of it. She was in love with Finn. And she was in love with Asher. Everything about her life was a total mess, and yet, she couldn't wish it any different. What choice would she make? Which option did she want taken away?

Asher—who had never done anything except love her? Or Finn—who set her on fire with passion, protected her in a weak moment, but walked away when she'd been set to choose him? Both sides of her heart were pulling against each other, rooting for different endings to her story. She'd never been so at war with herself.

"Finn—" She pulled away, their foreheads pressed together. He opened his eyes slowly as if dreading her next words. And honestly, she was dreading them, too. "I can't do this."

He nodded against her skin, backing away. "I know."

"I just...I'm engaged."

"Okay," he said.

"I'm sorry..." she whispered, unable to meet his eye.

"Yeah, well, me too." He grabbed hold of the door. "Take care of yourself, Blythe. Whatever you do, just... don't be afraid of the thing that makes you the happiest. Even if it's hard. Even if it's not me. Whatever makes you happy, you fight for it with all of your strength. Like you said, if you don't, what is the point of everything else?" He tapped the door. "Trust me, you don't want to live with that kind of regret."

She nodded, watching him open the door but unable to summon any words. Tears filled her eyes. "Finn, I—"

He stopped, looking back at her with slightly hopeful eyes. "It's okay," he said finally. "It doesn't have to be me. I'll be fine." His smile was small but warm.

"Thank you for everything."

"Anytime."

"I'm sorry..."

"You don't have to be."

"I know," she said. "But I am anyway."

With that, he shut the door and disappeared from her life—possibly for good.

CHAPTER TWENTY-THREE

TWO MONTHS LATER

"There," Blythe said. "The last of our invitations is officially done." She placed the seal over the flap to close it.

"I don't know if my fingers will ever straighten out completely again," Asher joked, holding out his hands as if they were claws.

She chuckled, leaning over onto his shoulder. "Thank you for helping me with this."

"Of course," he told her. "What better excuse to play hookie than to spend time with you? Even if it's doing the worst possible thing imaginable...which it was."

She wrinkled her nose at him. "I can't believe the wedding is almost here."

"It's flown by, hasn't it?" he asked. "I'm so ready to marry you."

"I know." She paused. "Your mother deserves to be a

professional wedding planner with all the work she's put into ours."

"I'm pretty sure she's been preparing for this event my whole life," he told her, smirking when she sat up off his shoulder. "This is her Olympics."

She smiled sadly, looking away.

"You're okay with it, right?" he asked. "I know she can be pushy."

"Of course," she agreed. "Your family is a godsend, Asher."

"But they make you miss yours," he said. It wasn't a question, but he was right.

She nodded. "They do."

He kissed her cheek. "I'm sorry, babe. I wish there was something I could do to make you feel better."

"You're already doing it," she told him. "You're amazing, Asher."

He shook his head. "I wish that was true."

"What do you mean?" she asked, sensing a strange tone in his voice.

"Just...you're the best thing I've ever done. I've made so many mistakes, Blythe."

"Mistakes?" She turned to face him on the couch. "What are you talking about?"

"I don't know." He groaned. "I never really thought I'd get here with my parents after all the craziness I put them through. In a lot of ways, it's like you repaired our relationship."

"I don't think that's true," she thought aloud. "Your family loves you."

"I know they do," he said. "I do."

"I do?" she repeated his words. "Now those words sound *amazing* coming out of your mouth."

"They do, do they?" he asked, a smile creeping onto his lips. "I'll bet they sound even better coming from yours." He ran a finger across her thigh, trailing it up her stomach in an attempt to tickle her. She let out a loud laugh, pushing him away, and he laughed, too. Then his face went serious after a moment. "You're without a doubt the best thing that's ever happened to me. I don't know how I'd ever survive losing you."

"You'll never have to," she assured him, taking his arm in her hand. "I love you."

"I love you, too," he told her, picking up the stack of envelopes and walking to lay them on his desk.

"Hey, Asher?" she asked.

He turned back to face her. "Yeah?"

"Why don't you work for your dad? Because of your past?"

He nodded. "Nobody wants someone with a past like mine managing their finances." He grimaced. "Besides, I wanted to do something for myself. I wanted my money, my things, to be my own. I never liked relying on my father to take care of me."

"I can understand that," she said, although it wasn't completely true. She never wanted more than her parents could give her, and they hadn't had nearly the money Asher had. "I just wondered. I mean, you're the only son. Does it bother him that you don't work for his company? He said a few of your cousins do."

He frowned. "We've never really talked about it. I think it's...tense, you know, obviously. But it is what it is."

She stood from the couch. "I like that you make your own money."

"I'm always going to take care of you, Blythe. You know that, right?" He took a step toward her, meeting her in the middle as she moved toward him.

"I do," she said, letting the all-powerful words slip from her tongue.

He smiled, leaning in for a slow kiss. "See, I was right. It sounds *much* better coming from you."

CHAPTER TWENTY-FOUR

TWO MONTHS LATER

Blythe stood in front of the long mirror at the church. The white gown hugged her curves, the ballgown skirt giving her princess vibes. She was wearing Grandmother Lorene's veil, a design on it that matched the ring she'd recently gotten back from being sized. The veil was beautiful, just like the ring, and so were the flowers Blythe and Mona had slaved over for months. Everything had come together in just seven months—the wedding of her dreams.

She hadn't heard from Finn since that night just four months ago. She'd spent the next week in her apartment telling Asher she needed to pack since she only had a few months left to get it done, but in reality, she was trying to make a decision that would shape the rest of her life.

She couldn't deny, even now in her dress, that Finn would possibly always have a piece of her heart. She'd given it to him unknowingly, and it was likely she'd never get it back. But Asher had the other half. He'd worked for it. He'd earned it. Asher didn't deserve to have his heart broken.

Not that Finn did, either. But Finn had chosen to leave. He'd chosen to hide his past rather than just be honest and take the risk. He'd made the choice for her, and at the end of the day, that was what mattered.

As she stared at herself in the mirror, at the perfect makeup and hair, the dress she never could've afforded before, and the ring that glistened on her finger, she couldn't help but be sad that her mother wasn't standing next to her. She was supposed to be, after all. This was a day they'd dreamed of for most of her life. She was supposed to wear her mother's veil, but it had burned up in the fire, like most of her belongings. Everything she'd owned had either been stolen in flames or ripped from her grasp the day she arrived in New York.

Everything about this day was fresh, new—just like the life she was walking into. It didn't feel the way she'd imagined it, but somehow that was okay. As long as she had Asher, as long as he loved her, everything would be okay.

"I wish you were here, Mom," she whispered, running a hand over her nervous stomach as her lip began to quiver. The next thought wasn't spoken aloud, but she hoped her mother could hear it anyway. *You'd know what to do.*

A knock on the door startled her, and she quickly brushed the tears from her eyes. Cathy, a girl she catered with and had chosen to be a bridesmaid, poked her head inside. "Hey, love, you about ready?"

She nodded. "Yeah."

"Okay, um, someone wants to see you first."

Her heart fluttered at the possibility. Who could it be? Rather, who *else* could it be? He shouldn't have come, but she couldn't deny the hope she felt at hearing her words. "Sure. Send them in."

She nodded, shutting the door for just a moment. When it opened, it was Jacob, not Finn, standing in front of her. The hope deflated from her chest like a balloon that had been popped. "Jacob," she said, trying to sound happier than she felt. "Everything okay?"

He shut the door before he responded. "You look beautiful."

She smiled at him, confusion coming out in her expression. "Thank you."

He cleared his throat. "I need to tell you something, Blythe. You can make of it what you will, and it's probably not my place to say anything, but I won't be able to live with myself if I don't."

"What are you talking about?" she asked, leaning against the white chaise lounge beside her. Her head pounded at the way he was looking at her. Something was very wrong.

"Finn told me about what happened between the two of you…er, the three of you, I guess. My son included."

Was he mad that she'd been in love with his son's friend? "I didn't know Finn and Asher were friends," she began to explain. "What Finn and I had was very brief, practically non-existent."

He smiled, holding a hand up to get her to stop talking. "You don't have to explain it to me, but there *is* something I want to explain to you."

Was it about money? Was this where he told her she'd have to sign a prenup? "Okay, sure."

"When Asher and Finn were growing up, they were inseparable. More like brothers than friends. Mona and I...well, to this day, we consider Finn our other son. We've taken care of him most of his life." He paused, pressing his lips together. "I'm not sure what all you know about Finn's upbringing..."

"Nothing." She answered the question he hadn't really asked.

He nodded. "It wasn't good. His parents are useless. His father is a big, mean man with a temper out of this world. He never had a kind thing to say to or about his son. His mother..." He raised his eyebrows. "His mother was on drugs his entire life. She had men in and out of Finn's life. When his father would run off for a month or two, she'd bring someone new home. There was no consistency. He turned out much better than we could've hoped for based on the people who raised him. Mona and I took him in when he was fifteen, after his mother over-dosed for about the fourth time and his father took off again." He looked away, and she wondered if she spied tears in his usually happy eyes. "They never even asked about him. For over a year, we had him and they didn't even realize he was gone."

"You did all you could for him," she said, unsure if she was supposed to be comforting him.

"No," he said softly, rubbing a thumb under his nose with a sniff. He looked back at her. "No, we didn't. I've always said I feel like I have two sons, but there was a time when they both needed me and I chose one over the other." He pinched the bridge of his nose. "I'll never forgive myself for that."

"What are you talking about, Mr. Grace?"

"Asher loves you, Blythe. He does. You have turned his life around since you walked into it, and his mother and I couldn't be more proud of that."

"I love him, too." She tilted her head toward her shoulder, waiting for him to go on.

"Mona would never forgive me if she knew I was here," he said, though it seemed like he was talking to himself more than her. "But you need to know the truth."

"The truth about what?" she asked.

"You need to talk to Finn," he said. "If you love him, too. If you care about Finn...you need to talk to him before you go through with this."

"Are you saying that I shouldn't get married today?" She touched her chest, trying to find a message within his guarded words.

"No," he said quickly. "I want you to marry my son more than I've ever wanted anything. You are the...*best* thing that has ever happened to him. But I can't be selfish this time. I can't choose one son over the other."

"I chose, Mr. Grace—"

"Jacob, Jack, please," he corrected her.

"Jacob," she said. "*Jack?*" Wheels in her mind began turning as she wondered why that rang a bell. "I've never heard anyone call you Jack."

"My father always did. Kids in school. Mona thinks it's childish, but I always liked it."

"Jack..." She thought back as the memory surfaced.

"Finn's father. Was he...bigger?" She held her arms out to her side. "A big, white beard?"

He nodded. "Yes, that's him."

"He came to Finn's apartment. A few weeks after I'd started dating Asher. Said you—Jack—told him where Finn lived." She nodded, feeling it all fall into place. "That's what you're talking about. You knew Finn would run away if his father found him. You knew he'd come to you and I'd go back to Asher."

He furrowed his brow. "No," he said softly. "No, of course not. I didn't know who you were at that time, Blythe. Let alone that you were dating both of my boys." He sighed. "I did tell Tommy where Finn lived, but only because he said he needed the address for a lawyer. Finn's mother passed away, and the will was being read. I asked Finn if it was okay, and he said yes. Neither of us expected that Tommy would show up there."

"So, if that's not what this is about, what are you talking about? When did you choose one son over the other?"

A knock on the door interrupted them, and Cathy stuck her head back in. "They're ready for us."

Blythe nodded, waiting for her to shut the door again before Jacob said anything else. "If you love Asher, and there are no doubts in your mind...then I hope you'll marry him. But, Blythe, if you have even one small doubt about going through with this...please talk to Finn first. I'm trying to protect all of my children here. That...that includes you." He smiled, walking forward and taking her hand. He pressed his lips to it, pulling her into a hug that made her miss her own father terribly. "Good luck," he whispered as he pulled away. "I'll stall for a few minutes if you need me to."

She nodded, but didn't accept or decline his offer at first. "I love Asher," she told him. "And he loves me too, right?"

He nodded. "He really does."

She smiled, despite the tears still in her eyes. "Is Finn here? Did he ask you to talk to me?"

"No," he said quickly. "Finn would never allow me to tell you all that I have. He didn't want me talking to you at all."

So, Finn hadn't chosen to fight for her. Again. He had given up. "Thank you for telling me what you have, Jack. I love your son, and he loves me. I don't have any doubts." The last sentence was a lie and she knew it as the words left her lips, but she couldn't take them back. She hugged the man in front of her again, turning toward the door. "Now, we've got a wedding to get to."

He looked incredibly relieved, though a bit troubled, as he pulled open the door. Blythe smiled as the three bridesmaids she'd chosen began to 'ooh' and 'aah' at the sight of her.

She entered the hallway as Cathy stuck her head through the large set of double doors to give the go-ahead. Instantly, the music started playing, letting them know the ceremony was starting.

Jacob started to take his place near the maid of honor but stopped and glanced back at Blythe.

"This may be overstepping…but would you like me to walk you down the aisle?"

His words slammed into her chest, causing her to suck

in a deep breath as the tears she'd been keeping mildly at bay began to pour down her cheeks. She hadn't mentioned to anyone how much this day made her miss her father. Everyone talked about missing her mother, how hard it must be for her to get married without her, and that was completely true, but she longed to wrap her arm through her father's in that moment. She had hidden the dismay she felt over the fact that there would be no father-daughter dance. Every part of this day was a reminder of what she had lost.

"I would love that very much," she said finally.

He stepped out of the way as the procession began making its way down the aisle. Asher would wonder why his father, his best man, wasn't with them. As the doors closed and it became their turn to walk down the aisle, Jacob leaned down close to her ear.

"I'm sure your father would be so proud of you." The doors opened, and Asher met her eyes from the end of the aisle. He smiled warmly, his eyes never leaving hers as they made their way toward him. The guests stood in unison, watching her with encouraging smiles on their faces. It wasn't lost on any of them that the entire crowd was filled with Asher's guests. A few of her friends from work had been invited, but excluding the three in her wedding party, none had bothered to come. Even her aunt, her only living family despite their tense relationship, had claimed it was too far a drive to attend.

She couldn't focus on that. No matter how sad it made her, the man waiting for her at the end of the aisle made her so incredibly happy she could burst.

When they reached Asher, Jacob placed her hand into

his son's before taking his place next to Asher as his best man.

"You look beautiful," Asher whispered, leaning in toward her slightly as they made their way up the red velvet staircase in front of the pastor. She smiled at him, her heart so incredibly full, and yet there was something bothering her. Jacob's words. The warning he'd given her. That she should talk to Finn. Why couldn't he have warned her before this moment?

She thought about the other thing he'd said to her, the one about her father being proud of her. Would he, though? As she looked around the room, the wedding that had been planned by well-meaning people, yet nothing looked as it would if she would've done it herself. The crowd was filled with unfamiliar faces.

The wedding felt like Asher's and Asher's alone, and though she had thought it wouldn't bother her, as she stood in front of strangers—her new family—she couldn't help missing her old family. She thought of the words her father had told her just before her graduation. He'd pulled her aside just before they'd gotten in the car.

"You know we're proud of you, right?" he'd said.

She'd rolled her eyes at the time. "Daaaad."

He'd kissed her forehead, squeezing her shoulder. "I know, I know. I'm just saying it now while I have you alone. After tonight, the world is yours, sweet pea. You can do and be anything you want."

She'd smirked. "You know I'm not, like, running off backpacking around Europe or something. I'm not even moving out yet."

"I know," he'd said. "But you could. This moment right

here is so full of possibilities. And the truth is, Blythe, as long as you follow your heart…you can't go wrong. Be true to yourself and what it will take to make you happy. Your mother and I will support you no matter what that is."

She'd leaned into his hug. "Thanks," she'd whispered. "Now, let's get going before we turn into a cheesy Hallmark movie."

He'd chuckled at her joke and walked with his daughter out the door. Her parents were dead just a few years later. She hadn't thought back to that day since then, hadn't remembered his advice until that moment. It was as if he knew she'd need to hear it someday.

Was she following her heart? As much as she wanted to believe she was as she stared at the man in front of her —the good man, the man who loved her more than anything else, the man who'd given her everything she thought she wanted—she knew it wasn't true. The piece of her heart that remained with Finn was too big. It had the majority vote, if she were being honest with herself. Maybe she'd always known it. Maybe the memory of her father on such an important day had forced that truth to the surface. Either way, she couldn't give up on him just because he so willingly conceded.

The pastor had made it through part of the ceremony and he was looking at her, waiting for her to say the words he was saying. Asher squeezed her hand.

"Blythe?" he whispered, looking confused. Her eyes met Jacob's, who gave her a knowing look. He'd known this would happen. Somehow, he'd just known.

"I, um—" She looked out into the crowd, trying to find

the words to say the very thing that would crush his heart more than anything else. It wasn't easy to destroy someone you loved, to destroy the future you pictured together. It was even more difficult to do so in front of a crowd of people who'd all come because they loved said person. Her eyes landed on a woman in the front row, all the blood draining from her face instantly.

It was the woman from the restaurant the night she and Asher had had their first fight. The girl he'd been dating at the same time as Blythe. She couldn't recall her name. As much as her presence shocked Blythe, that wasn't what made her heart race. She squinted her eyes, trying to determine if she was right. From such a distance, it was hard to tell. But she knew. In her heart, she knew, and yet, it wasn't possible. Was it?

She dropped Asher's hands quickly, walking toward the woman. The crowd gasped.

"What are you doing?" Asher asked.

The woman looked shocked; she scooted back farther on the pew without a word, trying to determine what was happening. As Blythe grew closer, her suspicions were confirmed.

She stared at the large, green emerald hanging from her neck, three smaller gems on either side. She'd know that necklace anywhere.

CHAPTER TWENTY-FIVE

"Where did you get that?" Blythe asked, her powerless voice carrying across the room. Asher was at her side in an instant, holding her shoulders.

"Sweetheart, what is it? What's wrong?"

"Where did you get that?" Blythe screamed, her power returning as anger filled her.

Jacob was at her other side. He cleared his throat. "Maybe we should take this to another room." He pulled Blythe, motioning that she and Asher should follow.

Mona stood up, her hand on her chest. "I'm so sorry about this, everyone," she announced. "You know how nerves go on a wedding day." The crowd chuckled half-heartedly. "We'll be right back, but please feel free to mingle." She hurried after them, her footsteps thudding on the red carpet that led down the aisle.

They arrived at the room in which Blythe had gotten dressed, and Blythe spun around, ready to rip the necklace from the pretty, tan neck of Asher's ex.

"Now, what is this all about?" Mona asked. It was the first time Blythe had seen her look even remotely angry.

Blythe pointed a finger at the woman, her hand and voice both shaking with fury. "Where...did...you...*get that?*"

"Blythe, what's going on?" Asher asked. "Bianca hasn't done anything—"

"*Where?!*" she squealed.

Bianca jumped, her hand flying to her necklace. "Asher gave it to me," she whispered. "Do you want it? I'm sorry. I just...I've always loved it. It doesn't mean anything."

Blythe choked back tears, holding out her hand as a terrified-looking Bianca reached behind her neck and unhooked the necklace, handing it over without a fight.

Asher looked at her as if she'd lost her mind—maybe she had. That was the only explanation that made sense. She turned the necklace over in her hand, the weight as familiar as the last time she'd held it. She looked at the back, the way the silver had begun to blacken with age, but yes, there they were. The initials she'd spent years tracing with her fingers. **AJ.**

"Where did *you* get it, Asher?"

"What are you talking about?" he asked, his brow furrowed.

She shoved the necklace into his face. "Where did you get my mother's necklace?"

His face went ashen instantly. "I, um, I bought it at a pawnshop."

"A pawnshop?" she asked. The possibility hadn't crossed her mind.

"Oh my God," Bianca said, covering her mouth. "No. Asher. Tell me you didn't."

Blythe had other things to worry about than whether Bianca was opposed to wearing pre-owned jewelry. "Which pawnshop?" she demanded.

"Um...the one..." He tried to think, his eyes trailing to the ceiling.

"Asher, you need to tell her the truth," Bianca said, her eyes darting to the necklace and then back to Asher.

"That is the truth," he insisted.

"If you don't, I will," Bianca told him, one brow raised.

"What's going on, Son?" Jacob asked, stepping up next to Blythe.

"I..." He looked at Bianca and then his father and then back to Blythe. His eyes fell to the ground, no words coming out of his mouth.

"Say it," Blythe demanded, already piecing together the truth but not wanting to believe it.

"Blythe, I—"

"Say it!"

When the answer came, it wasn't from Asher, but from Bianca. Her voice took the entire room by surprise. "You were the girl he mugged, weren't you?

CHAPTER TWENTY-SIX

B lythe ran through the church, holding the bottom of her dress up to keep from tripping, though it didn't seem to help as she stumbled for a second time. She hurried down the stairs, her makeup running, hair a frazzled mess. She had to get out of there. Had to get as far away as possible.

How could she have been so stupid? How could she have trusted a man who'd hurt her so badly? She carried her mother's necklace with a firm grasp. She'd never let go of it again if she had anything to say about it.

Stopping dead in her tracks as she stepped out of the large double doors, she let out a sound that was somewhere between a laugh and a cry.

As fast as his legs would carry him through the parking lot across from the church, Finn ran toward her. His hair flopped with each step, his mouth open as he sucked in deep breaths. The tux he'd worn was disheveled from the exertion, but nothing else mattered. He'd come for her. He was running to her. He'd chosen to fight at the very last moment it could matter. As his eyes met hers, a sorrowful look on his face, he froze. "Please...tell me... you...haven't married him," he said, huffing out breaths as he bent over his knees.

"I thought you weren't coming?" she asked softly, walking toward him.

"I couldn't let you do it, Blythe. Can't. Tell me...tell me you didn't."

She shook her head, reaching him finally. His eyes grew serious as he seemed to notice her tears. "I didn't marry him," she confirmed.

"You're crying. What's the matter?" he asked, taking her in his arms. "Are you okay?"

"No," she admitted, her voice cracking. "Can we just... go somewhere? Anywhere?"

"Where would you like to go?" he asked.

"Literally anywhere but here."

He walked around the car, pulling open the car door without another word and helping her climb inside. Once they were on the road, he looked at her again.

"What did he do?" he asked.

She bit her lip. How much was she ready to talk about? Truth be told, with anyone else, she would've said nothing. But this was Finn. Finn, who seemed to pull the truth out of her even when she wasn't ready to admit it to herself.

"Asher's the man who mugged me on the day we met." She picked at a piece of skin around her fingernail as she said the words.

He let out a soft growl that caused her to look up. Much to her surprise, he didn't look shocked.

"You knew?"

He shook his head, lowering his brow. "No, of course not. But I should have." His lips formed a tight, thin line as his fingers rolled over the steering wheel as if his grip was around Asher's neck instead.

"What are you talking about? How could you have known?"

"Is that necklace special to you?" he asked.

"It's all I have left of my mother," she said, running her fingers over the jewels. She could picture the many nights she'd spent waiting for the day it would get handed down to her, and the night it finally had, just before prom. "It was in my bag...it was the most important thing in my bag."

"Asher's always been a thief," Finn said frankly. "When we were kids, it was just petty stuff. Candy, magazines, whatever. But as we got older, it became more serious. He stole a car once. At least once that I know of, anyway. He'd dine and dash all the time. Steal expensive gifts for his girlfriends."

"But...I don't understand. He's rich. Why would he need to steal?"

He shrugged. "It's like...I don't know, a rush for him. A high without a needle. He'd have a bad day, and it was his way of blowing off steam. He wanted to have something of his own. His own money, his own stuff. Truth be told, that's probably why he didn't want to date you exclusively. He wants to collect whatever he can. He wants everything."

"But random muggings? Really?"

"I guess he's upped his game. Around the time I went

away, he'd gotten into some trouble for beating this kid in a parking lot over his wallet. The wallet had less than one hundred dollars in it. I tried to convince Asher to get help then. Rehab. Something. But…he just kept getting worse. Jack would always get him out of trouble, so he never had to face his own consequences."

"That's what he was talking about, then," she said, seeing it all come together. "Jack said he'd chosen Asher over you. Is that because he saved him from his crimes but couldn't help you?"

Finn shook his head. "Yeah, I guess so."

"But why would Asher want to date me? Marry me, even. Do you think he recognized me?"

"Honestly, Blythe, I have no idea. I don't see the point in that, but I don't know him anymore. He was a brother to me a long time ago, but he's practically a stranger to me now. I have no idea what's going on in his mind."

"If I hadn't seen this necklace, I'd be married right now. To someone who'd spent our entire relationship lying to me. I can't…" She took a deep breath, clutching her chest. "I can't believe how well he hid that part of himself from me. Am I just a complete idiot? Bianca knew. His father knew. You knew." She shook her head, her eyes wild.

"You aren't an idiot, Blythe. There are two very different sides to Asher, and he does well at keeping them separate. It's just like any other addiction, and he hid it from you because he didn't want you to see the bad parts of himself."

"Is that why you hid going to jail from me? To keep the version I see of you clean?"

He twisted his mouth in thought, turning the car onto a new street and sighing. "Blythe, I don't want to lie to you."

"So, don't."

"It's not that simple."

"What do you mean?"

"I'm not innocent," he said, placing his hand in the air. "I'm not. When Asher started stealing, I tried to get him to stop. But he was the rich kid and I was the one who grew up with nothing except what his parents could give me, so there were times when I joined in. He had all of this nice stuff to give to girls. I wanted that too. I never stole a car or anything that crazy, but I'm just saying…I'm not a white knight here."

"I don't expect you to—"

"Just…just listen, okay?" he said softly. "I need to get this out because what I'm about to tell you, I've never told another person. I've never spoken it out loud."

"What is it?" she asked, sensing the seriousness of his tone.

"One night after school, we went to this bar using fake IDs that Asher had scored for us from some friend of his father's. We thought we were hot shit, walking in there like we belonged." He scoffed. "Later that night, he found me at the bar. He had two girls that he said we were going to party with. They were older. Twenties, I guess. He said we could go back to their apartment." He rolled his eyes. "As we were leaving, Asher had the girls wait out front and told them we had to get something first. I thought he'd stolen from them and we were about to leave. He had been texting all night, but I didn't think much of it until

180

we got to the corner of the alley and his dealer was there." He spoke slowly, contorting his mouth as she watched him attempt not to lose his composure. "He owed him some money, but he thought he could score something to hold him over. Asher wasn't used to being told no."

"But the Graces are rich. Why wouldn't he just pay him?"

"Asher was too proud to ask his dad for money when things got tough. It's why he doesn't work for him. He benefited from their wealth, but he always wanted to do things his way. He didn't work through most of college, so money was scarce. His parents paid his bills, but he blew through allowances as quickly as they came and wouldn't ask for more."

"So what happened?" she asked, her mouth open as she listened in disbelief to the nightmare Finn was laying out. "With the dealer?"

"I told Asher he was crazy. I told him we didn't need anything and that we should call his dad and get it all paid off before anything had to happen. The dealer was furious. Asher had wasted his time coming there with no money and asking for more. I couldn't let him do it."

"That was the dealer that you killed? For Asher?"

He wouldn't look at her as he went on. "I never killed him. I offered to pay him. I told him I'd borrow the money from Asher's parents myself if I had to. I wanted to go warn the girls to leave, in case the guy got too mad. He wasn't having it. Asher owed him a lot of money, and he said we weren't leaving until we paid him what Asher owed. I knew Asher smoked weed and took a few pills now and again, but I had no idea what all he was into."

"So, what happened?"

"He pulled a gun on me, told me to shut up or he'd kill me. Asher lunged at him—like an idiot—and the gun went off. His head hit the wall. Just like that and it was over." He snapped his fingers. "I always thought death would be more dramatic but he was just…gone."

"*Asher* killed him?"

He nodded. "Protecting me."

"From a situation *he* caused. You shouldn't have gone to jail for that." She paused. "Wait a second, *that's* what Jacob meant, isn't it? He chose Asher over you."

Finn sighed. "We didn't have a choice. The gun went off and people were coming, so we ran. We ran like hell, and we made it away that night. But the girls told police that we'd been down that alley. When they came looking for us, wanting to know what had happened…Jack made me a deal."

"What kind of deal?" she asked.

"I took the blame for everything. Said Asher wasn't involved."

"But why?"

"Because he promised to take care of my mom."

"Your mom?" She swallowed, her throat tight. After all Jacob had said about Finn's parents, why would Finn want to take care of them?

"Judging by that expression, you must know she was never parent-of-the-year material, but she tried, Blythe. She really did. When she was sober. When she wasn't getting the crap beaten out of her by my old man."

"So, you signed away your life to protect your parents? Just like that?"

"Not just like that. It took some convincing. But I was loyal to Asher. He'd saved my life. If it weren't for him, I may not have even had a life to sign away."

"If it weren't for him, you wouldn't have been in that situation in the first place."

"Maybe so," he admitted. "But it is what it is."

"And Asher was okay with that? He just let you go away for what he'd done?"

"Jack hired the best possible lawyer. He fought for me. I don't know what Asher knew. Jack told me he was going to send him out of state for college, that he'd tell him he was taking care of everything. He thought Asher may try to stop him if he knew the truth."

"Do you think he would've?" At least there was a speck of goodness in the man she'd almost married.

"I don't know," he admitted. "I honestly don't. I'd like to think so."

"But...why wouldn't you warn me about him? Why would you let me marry him?"

"I didn't want you to think I was telling you not to be with him for selfish reasons. There was no way I could tell you to leave him, tell you any of this, and not have you thinking it was because I wanted you for myself. I wanted you to want to be with me because I was who you liked, not because I'd painted Asher in a bad light and aired out his secrets. And, besides, as far as I knew, Asher had turned his life around. I kept in contact with Jacob over the years. Getting out of New York was supposed to have really worked well for Asher. He'd been out of trouble all this time. I chose to believe that night changed him."

"I can't believe this," she said, the weight of the story

hitting her. How on earth could anyone hide this much of who they were? How could Asher have held onto this secret for so long? She could see the weight Finn still carried—the guilt. "It's not your fault, you know. He saved you because he put you in a horrible situation. He's not a good person, Finn. He's not. If not for him, think about how different your life could've been."

"I don't know," he said, the slyness to his voice back. "I kind of like my life now. Besides, if not for him, I'd never have met you."

She grimaced at the thought but looked down at the necklace. She couldn't thank Asher for bringing Finn into her life, but she could thank her mother. Her mother who had led her to New York, had brought Finn into her life the day the necklace had been torn from her grasp, and her mother who, on the day she was set to make the biggest mistake of her life, had shown up one last time to reveal the truth. She raised the necklace to her chest, hugging it and wishing she could feel her mother's arms around her neck once more. *Thank you, Mama.*

"Speaking of," she said, going back to his last words, "were you just planning to hang around outside in case I changed my mind?"

"A guy can hope, can't he?" He smiled sadly, reaching for her hand. "Are you okay?" he asked, his tone serious.

She felt a small tear trickle down her cheek. She wasn't okay. Of course she wasn't. The plan she had for her life just an hour ago, had been ripped to shreds in front of her eyes. But at least she knew the truth. At least she knew before it was too late. "I will be," she promised. "Thanks to you."